D0841701

Stonewall Inn Mysteries
Keith Kahla, General Editor

The Donald Strachey Mysteries
by Richard Stevenson

Richard Stevenson

CHAIN OF FOOLS

A Donald Strachey Mystery

Withdrawn

St. Martin's Press ❧ *New York*

Library of Congress Cataloging-in-Publication Data

Stevenson, Richard
        Chain of fools / by Richard Stevenson.
            p.   cm.
        "A Donald Strachey mystery."
        ISBN 0-312-16796-2
        I. Title.
    PS3569.T4567C48   1996
    813'.54—dc20   96-25586
                                            CIP

First Stonewall Inn Edition: November 1997

10   9   8   7   6   5   4   3   2   1

LA-1999-5-1

For Sydney and Zack

1

One's a good chain and one's a bad chain," Skeeter Mc-Caslin eerily intoned from his hospital bed. "One's a daisy chain and one's a chain of fools." His dark eyes were bright with fever, and he looked suspicious and terrified and cunning all at the same time.

Timothy Callahan and I glanced at each other over our gauze masks, then looked back at Skeeter.

"But when you called the other day," Timmy said, "you told me a friend's life was in danger—a woman at the newspaper in Edensburg. Why don't you tell Don and me about that, Skeeter? You were right to call. I'm really glad you did, because Don might be able to help."

Skeeter's jaw tightened under his stubble of black beard, the whiskers an indication not of fashion but of illness, and he scowled. "I just *told* you, didn't I? Now I am going to tell you *one . . . more . . . time.* One's a good chain, and one's a bad chain. One's a daisy chain, and one's a chain of fools."

After a little pause, Timmy said, "Chain of fools?"

Skeeter did not rise up from his pillow—he was obviously far too sick and exhausted for that—but he cocked a bushy eyebrow and said, in a voice dripping acid, "Do I have to repeat myself a *third* time? One's a—"

"I'll be right back," Timmy said. He got up and walked out into the corridor.

I said to Skeeter, "Your friend who's in danger—is her name Aretha?" His eyes burned with contempt. I was a moron. I asked, "Is it Buchanan? As in Daisy Buchanan?"

"You're an even bigger idiot than your boyfriend is," Skeeter said.

He gave me a look indicating that I was as useful to him, and as appealing, as the uneaten dun-colored roast beef and bile-green string beans on the dinner plate at his bedside.

"Skeeter, I have a feeling you're not yourself tonight," I said. "Timmy always spoke well of you, and I hope we can get to know each other when you're feeling better. Then we can sort this thing out—whatever the situation is that led you to believe that your friend might be in need of a private investigator. Okay?"

Skeeter grinned dementedly. He said, "Did Timmy tell you about my birthmark?"

"Nope. Never did."

"Timothy sure did love that birthmark."

"Good."

Timmy came back into the room, trailing a nurse. She barged over to Skeeter, peered at the numbers on his IV-drip monitors, jiggled something, and said loudly, "Mr. McCaslin, how ya doin'?"

Skeeter replied, "One's a good chain, and one's a bad chain."

"Oh, is that so?"

"One's a daisy chain, and one's a chain of fools."

"Uh-huh. Hmm." Now she was examining the label on one of the drip bags. She said to Skeeter, "How long have you been on this?"

"Planet?"

"No, this prednisone."

"Forty-eight hours," Skeeter said.

"Oh, yeah?"

"That was before the admission into the union of Alaska and Hawaii. But I still stand up and salute when I'm not sick as a dog."

"Well, they might have to change this one med. I'll have to talk to the doctor about it. Who's your attending? Baptiste?"

"I'm just a simple forest ranger from Edensburg. I call him Baptist. Or Evangelical Lutheran."

"Uh-huh."

"One's a good chain, and one's a bad chain. One's a daisy chain, and one's chain of fools."

"Well, you have a nice visit with your friends." The nurse turned and sped away, and Timmy sped after her.

Skeeter looked over at me balefully and waited.

I said, "Where's the birthmark?"

2

"Wouldn't you like to know. Wouldn't you *just* like to know."

"Timmy considers himself lucky to have hooked up with you, Skeeter. For most gay kids, high school is hell. I'm sure it was hard in a lot of ways for you too—not feeling as though you could be open about your relationship and all that. But at least you two knew exactly who you were and what you wanted, and you had each other. That's unusual."

He stared at me as if I had spoken to him in Gheg. After a moment, he said, "One's a good chain, and one's a bad chain. One's a daisy chain, and one's a chain of fools."

"I got that, Skeeter. I just wish I had a clue as to what the hell you're talking about."

"You know what I'm talking about, Donald. You know *damn* well. Oh, ho ho."

Timmy returned. "Skeeter," he said, "you're on a steroid drug that's affecting your mind. Now that the pneumocystis is under control, maybe they can change the medication. The nurse is going to check."

"It's *your* mind that's affected, not mine," Skeeter said. "You could cut my heart out, the way you did the last time, and plead temporarily asinine."

"I think maybe we should come back tomorrow," Timmy said, his face coloring. "And then you'll be in better shape to talk about whatever you called me for on Thursday. Would I be wasting my breath if I asked you one more time to explain to Don and me about the good and bad chains, and how they're connected to your friend whose life may be in danger?"

Skeeter said, "Boo hoo, what a waste."

"Gotcha. I guess we'll head out then."

"I'm glad I finally got to meet you, Skeeter," I said. "I know it means a lot to Timmy too to be reconnected with you after all these years."

"Still crazy," Skeeter said.

I asked, "When was the last time you two saw each other?"

Skeeter said, "September second, 1963, four-twenty A.M. I still have his taste in my mouth."

Timmy blushed some more and said, "You've got a mighty long memory, Skeeter, or poor habits of oral hygiene. Anyway, you and I can do some catching up when you're feeling better. Which will be soon, I hope. I want to hear all about your life in the wilderness. I think that's great—all you ever wanted to be, when we were kids, was a forest ranger, and that's what you went ahead and did. I'm impressed. Maybe even a little envious."

"Now you're impressed. Then you were undressed."

Timmy said, "Skeeter, your tact mechanism is on the blink, so I think Don and I will be going now. There's no point in our hanging around any longer tonight. We'll come back this time tomorrow and with any luck you'll be better equipped to explain why you think your friend's situation is dangerous. I hope you can get a good night's rest. Hospitals certainly aren't restful places. In that sense, they're terrible places to have to go when you're ill."

"They killed Eric and now they're trying to kill Janet," Skeeter said in a matter-of-fact way.

Timmy had given Skeeter's arm an affectionate squeeze and was preparing for his exit, but now he stared down at the man he called his "old high-school friend." On those rare occasions when he mentioned Skeeter McCaslin at all to me, Timmy had never used the term "lover." He'd once said it was too suggestive and sophisticated a word for a couple of sex-crazed adolescents in early-Beatles-era Poughkeepsie. Yet their two-year affair, which ended only when they graduated from high school, was carried on with high degrees of both stealth and emotional heat. If "lovers" was too grown-up a term for what Timmy and Skeeter had been to each other, "friend," or even "sexual friend," was clearly insufficient. "Boyfriend" wasn't right either—this was more than a decade before same-sex couples began showing up at the proms together. On this point, the language was as inadequate as the times had been.

Timmy let go of Skeeter and gazed down at him uneasily. The man in the bed was gaga—temporarily, we'd been assured—and assigning meaning to his utterances, or inviting additional ones, seemed risky.

Boldly, I said, "Who was Eric, Skeeter? And who is Janet—the one they are trying to kill?"

"And while you're at it," Timmy added, "who are 'they'?"

"One's a good chain," Skeeter said, "and one's a bad chain. One's a daisy chain, and one's a chain of fools."

Timmy said, "Skeeter, I guess you can't help it, but saying that over and over is not useful. I think we're going to have to wait until your mind clears. Listen, old friend, we'll be back tomorrow. So you just hang in there and—"

"Eric was my lover," Skeeter said, "for eleven years. Eric Osborne, the famous eco-freak and prize-winning nature writer. When Eric won a Polk, he even knew who Polk was. To me, Polk was a pig in a poke. I said, 'Who's Polk?' and Eric knew. Eric knew puh-lenty. Eric knew me, ho ho—read me like a book, wrote me in a book. And I knew Eric like a mountain knows a polecat. Eric was the second great love of my life. But they killed him, on May the fifteenth, and now I'm going to die alone."

As he said this, a big, blue-eyed, long-faced woman with freckles and a sun-bleached mess of straw-colored hair strode into the room. From behind her surgical mask, she said, "Eldon, you are neither alone nor dying, just having a little psychotic episode. But you'll get over it. Hi," she said, offering Timmy, then me, a latexed hand. "I'm Janet Osborne, a friend of Eldon's."

"One's a good chain, and one's a bad chain. . . ."

"I'm Timothy Callahan, an old high-school friend of Eldon's."

"One's a daisy chain, and one's a chain of fools. . . ."

"Don Strachey—I'm with Timothy. Are you one of the *Edensburg Herald* Osbornes?"

"I edit the paper. Are you the private investigator? Eldon told me his high-school main squeeze was now the partner of a private detective and he was planning on contacting you."

"I was Eldon's only squeeze in high school," Timmy said, "unless you count Carol Jean Nugent in ninth grade. Right, Skeeter?"

The man in the bed said, "Guilty. Guilty as charged."

"Eldon, I never knew you had such an adorable nickname when you were a kid. Was Eric aware that you were once a Skeeter?"

"The wearin' o' the green," Skeeter said.

"And you work for the legislature, is that right, Timothy?"

"For Assemblyman Lipshutz."

"Eldon said he'd once read a piece in *Cityscape* about the two of you—a well-known gay-couple-about-Albany—and when he decided that I might be in need of a private eye, he remembered you two. Though my suspicion is, he mostly wanted to satisfy his curiosity about what had become of his first great love."

"Timmy popped my cherry real good," Skeeter said. "I cannot tell a lie."

"I didn't even know Skeeter was in the area," Timmy said. "We hadn't been in touch at all since high school."

"Instead of staying with me, he gave himself to the Mother Church," Skeeter said. "What he gave me was the Poughkeepsie royal kiss-off."

"By that, Skeeter means I went off to Georgetown, where I majored in political science."

Skeeter said, "Now it's thirty-two years later and he's still the all-American Irish hunk with milk-white skin and hair as soft as eiderdown, and me, I'm a dead duck."

"Eldon, you're a long way from dead," Janet said, "and the nurse says you're making steady progress."

"Quack, quack."

I said, "Eldon called Timmy before he got sick last week and told him he had a friend in Edensburg whose life was in danger. Apparently he meant you, Janet."

She gave a quick nod. "I suppose we should talk about that. We could go somewhere—or it could wait until tomorrow."

"They killed Eric, and now they're trying to kill Janet," Skeeter said. "One's a good chain, and one's a bad chain. One's a daisy chain, and one's a chain of fools."

"Eric was my brother," Janet said. "He was a writer. Eldon and Eric were together for eleven years. Eric died in May. He was murdered. We were all devastated, but no one more than Eldon. To lose someone you love that way—it's just the absolute hellish worst." Janet Osborne was a youthful and robust-looking woman, but when she spoke of her brother's murder something in her face altered, and it occurred to me that she was not as young as I had first thought.

"Don and I both read Eric's books," Timmy said. "He was a wonderful writer. His love of the Adirondacks was so infectious that every time either of us read Eric, we'd plan a camping trip the first chance we got to try to see the wilderness the way he saw it. Once, after we read Eric's article in *Harper's* about his winter week on Berry Pond, we decided to spend a February weekend there ourselves. Although I have to admit we spent the second night at the Edensburg Travelodge."

"Couple of nellies," Skeeter said. "Timmy, do tell me: Is it still your habit to take three showers a day?"

6

"No, Skeeter, I make do with two now that I'm middle-aged and am called upon to perspire less often than when I was younger."

"Living with me has turned Timothy into a big slob," I said.

"I was sure your skin would be all dried out from washing your natural body oils down the drain three times a day for forty-some years, but your skin's not hideous at all. I don't know why. You're almost totally bald in the back though."

"Skeeter, I would have expected that as a forest ranger you'd have progressed to concerns less fleeting than those of mere human vanity."

"Oh, so now you're into enemas. I could have predicted this."

"What?"

Janet said, "Eldon, I think we'd better leave you now, and you can get a good night's rest—or a bad night's rest if that's the best anybody can manage around here. I'll come back tomorrow night and see how you're doing, and some of the forest service gang is planning to come by too. The nurse thinks you ought to be okay, especially if they can get you off this prednisone. You're probably clinically insane, which as far as I know is not what the doctor ordered."

"Call me Olivia."

Timmy said, "So long, Olivia."

"I hated you for leaving me," Skeeter suddenly spat out. "I was so mad at you I could have killed you." He started to breathe fast and hard. This was bad, I was sure, for a man recovering from a lung disease.

Looking stricken, Timmy said, "Oh."

Skeeter gasped out, "I went up in the woods past Peterson's Bluff and screamed my head off. I pulled trees out by the roots. I cursed your name, Timmy. I despised you. I crushed your skull with rocks. When I got to forestry school, I cried half the night before I fell asleep. I lied to the other guys and told them my mother had died."

"Oh. Oh, Skeeter. God."

"I loved you and hated your guts for years, Timmy." Timmy looked away. "I never really got completely over you until I met Eric," Skeeter said, glaring at Timmy.

Timmy flushed scarlet and said, "All those years. Jeez, Skeeter. I'm sorry."

"Then and only then were you kaput, Callahan."

"Oh."

"And then it was Eric and I—in for however long it lasted, what with our HIV. Till ridiculous death do us part."

"I'm so sorry."

"I'm the one that got sick first."

"That was awful."

"But at least I still had Eric along for the idiotic ride—until they killed him."

"Who are 'they'?" Timmy said, seizing on this turn in the conversation toward behavior that was even more reprehensible in Skeeter's mind than Timmy's had been.

"That's what your boyfriend has to find out. Who *they* are. I can tell you this: They're in it with the bad chain."

I said, "The chain of fools?"

"Yes, yes, yes, yes."

"The business about the chains is still unclear to us, Skeeter. We might have to come back tomorrow to get that part of the story straight."

Janet said, "I can explain what Eldon is talking about. The *Herald* is on the verge of bankruptcy, and the family is being forced to sell out. One newspaper chain that's interested has made a low bid, but the advantage is that it would maintain the paper's high standards and progressive editorial page, especially on environmental matters. That's the good chain. The high bidder is a big chain run by a reactionary thug who would fire most of the staff, gut the paper editorially, and use it primarily as a vehicle for chain-store advertising. I guess that's the chain of fools. Some members of my family want to sell to the thug and walk away with a bundle. Others want to sell to the good chain, break even, and keep the Osbornes' good name. One vote for the good chain was lost when Eric was murdered. Someone may be trying to kill me—this is Eldon's theory—and eliminate my vote for selling out to the good chain. With my vote lost, the reactionary thug would win." A sheen of perspiration was visible now across Janet's forehead and around her pale eyes.

"Do you have any reason to believe that Eldon's theory is correct?" I asked.

"I'm not sure," Janet said. "I hate to think that any of the Osbornes would murder someone else in the family for money, or for anything else, or would ever murder anybody for any reason. But, I also know

8

that—let's just say for now that what Skeeter is suggesting might be possible." She gave a wan little shrug, as if to apologize for any homicidal tendencies in the Osborne family.

Skeeter said, "They sent the Jetsons to attack her. Betski-wetski. Honk honk, she almost got conked."

Timmy looked blankly at Skeeter, but Janet seemed to know what this meant. "Last week somebody might have tried to run me over with a Jet Ski," she said. "On the lake where I live. That's what Skeeter is referring to in his overly colorful way."

"Might have?" Timmy asked.

"There are a certain number of hotdoggers on the lake, so it *could* have been carelessness," Janet said, looking grim. "Or it could have been deliberate. We just don't know."

"One's a good chain, and one's a bad chain. It was almost a tall doll with a fractured skull," Skeeter said, and rolled his eyes up inside his head and made his tongue loll idiotically. That's when we all agreed it was time for Skeeter to get some rest.

2

"She was determined to stay calm—I'll bet she's a real rock—but you could see that Janet Osborne is frightened," Timmy said later, as we walked back toward our house on Crow Street.

A big red moon with an enormous blotch shaped like Sri Lanka hung in the eastern sky, and the August night air was as thick as black tea. As we headed down Madison, the Victorian-revival apartment buildings on our side of the street could have been overlooking an Indonesian waterfront instead of Washington Park. It was tropical Albany at its most intoxicating until we got to the donut shop at the corner of Lark, where the light was cold fluorescent and the smell was of powdered sugar and jelly filling and the illusion was lost.

"Families are supposed to be safe havens from the violence and irrationality of the larger world," Timmy said. "To suspect somebody in your own family of killing somebody else in the family must feel like having your soul poisoned."

I said, "Homicide is not one of the family values Pat Robertson would encourage, as a rule, but it does crop up from time to time. And that's not counting, of course, all the subtler intrafamily assassinations that don't involve bloodshed and therefore aren't against the law."

"Operating a family business must be particularly tricky," Timmy said, "since business decisions have to be fairly hardheaded and Freudian undercurrents can only muck things up. And then when the business starts to fail, all kinds of old family furies must be let loose."

"According to the literature—so I've heard—family businesses tend to fall apart, if they're going to, when the third generation takes over," I said. "The first generation founds the business, the second builds and secures it, and then the third-generation fuckups arrive and run the whole thing into the ground. The Osbornes are not unique in this, although there's something especially ugly about a newspaper of the *Herald*'s history and caliber being wrecked as if it were just a thoughtlessly situated Chinese takeout."

"How did the *Herald* end up near bankruptcy, anyway? Edensburg's economy should be solid—tourism and the canoe factory are both holding up—and there's no other paper up there to compete in any serious way."

We turned off busy Madison Avenue and onto cozy Crow Street, with its brick sidewalks and historically beplaqued town houses. "I'll find out more about the *Herald* when I meet with Janet tomorrow," I said. "But I know newspapers everywhere in the country are having a tough go of it with newsprint costs way up and ad revenues being drained off by junk mail, shoppers' guides, cable TV, and whatever else is hurtling down the information superhighway toward us."

"The trouble with the information superhighway," Timmy said, "is that it's a brave new highway mostly carrying the same tired information, and worse. And it's destroying institutions like the *Herald,* where the quality of the information is still considered more important than the extent of the profits that are piled up delivering it." A thoughtful pause. "I guess I'm beginning to sound like a fogy. Don, am I becoming a fogy?"

"You were always a fogy."

"I forgot."

"Gramps Callahan."

"Gramps when not Grumps."

"Except, Timothy, your fogyism is appropriate in this case—as it is, I've noticed as I get older, on any number of occasions. Commercial enterprises with social consciences are getting swallowed up by soulless conglomerates with superior technology, big bucks, and a habit of tossing workers by the thousands out on the street. And the *Edensburg Herald,* if it's grabbed, will represent a classic example of the trend. It stinks. If somebody in or outside the Osborne family is using murder to hurry the process along, I'd like to interfere if I can."

"Good."

"You know, it was interesting tonight to be reminded of how *un*fogylike you were in your last two years of high school, Timothy. Your information superhighway sure was humming back then."

"Well, that's about what it amounted to—neurons and glands working overtime."

"Neurons and glands and hydraulics."

"Those too."

"Poor Skeeter. For him it wasn't just teenage lust, it's now apparent."

"No."

We crossed Hudson Avenue, where the streetlight was aswarm with tiny insects. "Weren't you a little rattled by Skeeter's display tonight?" I asked. "It is not in your nature to intentionally bring emotional pain to another human being. I guess you didn't know—back in '63—just how smitten Skeeter was with you."

Looking straight ahead, Timmy said, "I knew."

We walked on, but I could feel him tense up beside me. A little farther down the block, he said, "The trouble was, see . . . I couldn't face it."

"No."

"Being a faggot, I mean."

"I knew what you meant."

"Skeeter wanted us to keep on being—sexually infatuated was what it was for me. For him it was more. I was only in love with sex, but Skeeter was in love with me. He wanted to write, and phone, and visit me in D.C., and for me to visit him in Plattsburg and for us to spend our vacations together. I broke it off partly because I had mixed feelings about Skeeter as a person—he was always just a little too emotionally erratic for me. But mainly I broke off the relationship—it's as clear to me now as it was back then—because Skeeter was a homosexual, and if I stayed with him that would mean I was a homosexual too."

"Yuck. Arrgh."

"So I broke it off."

"You never saw him again?"

"I didn't accept his phone calls in the dorm, I didn't answer his letters, I didn't go home for Thanksgiving, and at Christmas I faked the flu and never left the house. He phoned twice a day for three weeks, and I told Mom I was too sick to come to the phone. Actually, I was in my room writing a paper on Teilhard de Chardin and reading *City*

13

of Night, which was camouflaged inside the cover of *A Stone for Danny Fisher.* Talk about confused."

"Your parents never caught on?"

"I'm sure they were baffled, and worried. They could see that I wasn't all that sick. I'm sure I was consuming an awful lot of baloney sandwiches with mayonnaise for a flu victim."

"And then there was Skeeter baying outside your window. It must have been hellish for him. For both of you."

"It was."

We came to the house and Timmy, his key out of his pocket and aimed like a derringer for the previous half block, led the way in.

"I imagined," Timmy said, "that after Christmas, when Skeeter finally stopped calling and writing, he'd found somebody else. At least that's what I made myself think." We headed for the kitchen, where I got a beer from the fridge, and Timmy said, "I guess I'd better have one too." We pried open the back door, abloat in the wet heat, and sat out on the moonlit deck with the petunias.

I said, "If you imagined Skeeter with someone else, weren't you jealous?"

"Absolutely. It was excruciating. But I was only getting what I deserved, I believed. And I was right. In fact, after what I'd done to Skeeter I deserved even worse."

"Nah."

"I did."

"You only did what a lot of people do at the end of adolescence and the beginning of adulthood: You leave your childhood sweetheart because you're both about to become grown-ups, and your lives and circumstances are going to be different. It's hard and it's cruel, but it's a necessary part of life."

"No," Timmy said, "the main reason I cut Skeeter off was I was afraid of not being normal. Mainly, not being *thought of* as normal."

"Yes, but that's all you did in the name of normality—end a high-school infatuation. You didn't—you weren't like Jean-Louis Trintignant in *The Conformist.* You didn't commit murder for the fascists in order to fit in."

Timmy raised his bottle. "Well, let's drink to that. No, at least I didn't do that—assassinate a liberal for the fascists. At least, as far as I can recall I didn't."

14

We drank.

I said, "And however much you may have rejected abnormality back in the sixties, Timothy, you certainly made up for it in the seventies. As so many of us did." I gestured salaciously.

Timmy didn't seem to notice this. Gazing at the red moon, he was deep in thought. Finally, he said, "I can never undo what I did to Skeeter back then. It's obvious that the pain I caused him was so deep and terrible that it will be a part of him until he dies. And it's going to make his dying too young even worse than it would have been, which is mean and stupid enough."

"Timmy, you're being far too hard on yourself."

"But you know," he said, giving me a weird, feverish look I wasn't sure I had ever seen on him before, "maybe I can make it up to Skeeter in a small way. I can do this by helping with the thing that's most important to him now: by finding out who killed Eric, and by keeping Janet safe if she's in any actual danger. And by saving the *Herald* from the bad chain, the chain of fools."

He had lit a citronella candle to keep the bugs away, and its light flickered across his fine-featured Irish mug and in his suddenly brighter eyes. He seemed almost possessed by this sudden notion, which to me felt vaguely but surely like trouble.

I said, "Hey, Timothy. I'm the detective, and you're the pragmatic but idealistically motivated social engineer. Remember?"

This didn't seem to register. "I'll hire you," he said, "and I'll take time off from work—the Assembly is in the August doldrums now—and I'll help you out. Anyway, Don, you're—'between projects' is the euphemism, I believe. It's something we can do together, and it's something I can do for Skeeter. One last thing."

I thought this over, but not for long. "Timothy, I don't know. Your impulse is worthy. It's your decent heart asserting itself. But as for our working together, that sounds risky. Often you don't like the way I operate. My methods have sometimes left you despondent. Outraged, even. The whole thing could become . . . awkward."

His face glowed in the strange moonlight. He said, "I'll take that chance. I certainly can't think of anybody I'd rather hire than you, Don."

"No, Timmy, you can't think of anybody you'd rather share a roll of dental floss with than me. Detective-client relationships are different. Anyway, Skeeter might want to hire me, or Janet Osborne might.

Either would make a lot more sense. This whole business of Eric's unsolved murder being connected to any possible attempts on Janet's life is highly speculative. Janet wasn't all that sure that the so-called Jet Ski attack that Skeeter was blithering about was even an attack on her at all. I'll talk to Janet tomorrow—I've agreed to do that with no charge or obligation to anybody. But how about if we just take this thing one step at a time?"

"Okay," he said, "but if it's all right with you, I think that tomorrow I'll just come along for the ride. We can decide later on who'll pay."

This was unprecedented. This was not good. I said, "Well, I think you just *won't* come along for the ride tomorrow. Timmy, even if you were my client, I don't generally take clients along while I'm working on an investigation. They tend to get in the way, and you would not want to do that. Look, how about if I don't come to work with you and you don't come to work with me? How's that?"

"I've helped you out plenty of times," he said levelly, "and on cases that were just as murky in the beginning as this one is. I've done my share of cleaning up the murk. I've never—as you put it—gotten in the way. Admit it. Have I? I have only been helpful—sometimes extremely helpful—and occasionally in dangerous and ugly situations."

"This is different," I said, knowing exactly where this was heading. "You are emotionally involved."

"Well, of *course,* I'm emotionally involved," he said, throwing up the hand that wasn't tightly clutching a bottle of beer. "Skeeter is going to die, for God's sake! And since I hurt Skeeter very badly at the beginning of his adult life, I think I owe it to him to make things easier, if I can, at the end of his life. I'm in a position to help Skeeter and ease my own guilty conscience over the hell I put him through thirty-two years ago. And damn it, Don, I want to do it!"

I thought, Skeeter, Skeeter, Skeeter, Skeeter.

3

The *Edensburg Herald* had been founded in 1895, when young Daniel Lincoln Osborne, a fire-in-the-moral-soul Eugene Debs progressive, borrowed $11,000 from Hiram Young, his father-in-law, a foundry owner esteemed for his fair-labor practices, and merged two weekly newspapers of no particular distinction into the town's first daily. The new paper soon made a name for itself—not a good one, according to local mossback Republicans. From the beginning, the *Herald* railed against the depredations of the robber barons, supported labor and trustbusters, and was passionate in its editorials favoring the preservation of the Adirondacks' water, air, wildlife, and rugged natural beauty. It was almost single-handedly responsible for the creation of six state and two national parks, one containing what is now Lake Osborne, New York, and another Osborne Falls.

Later, the *Herald* welcomed FDR's New Deal, which the Eden County Republican Committee branded "the triumph of the Bolsheviks." When Hiram Young was in his eighties, he was still shunned by Edensburg families prominent in banking, real estate, and canoe manufacturing who never forgave him for bankrolling his son-in-law's renowned and apparently indestructible purveyor of—in the words of the president of the Eden County Savings Bank—"socialist hog offal."

The paper won its first of three Pulitzers, just before old Dan's retirement in 1945, for its editorials urging the formation of the United Nations. The second came during the Vietnam war, when Dan's son and successor, William T. "Tom" Osborne, drove Lyndon Johnson to distraction with antiwar screeds so elegantly incisive that papers all over the country regularly reprinted them, and Frank Church and J. William

Fulbright read them aloud on the floor of the U.S. Senate. The *Herald*'s third Pulitzer, ten years later, went to Eric Osborne for the "Letter from the Wilderness" reports that ceased only when he died the previous May, bludgeoned to death on one of the mountainsides he had so lustrously vivified for his readers.

Eric's was the most recent addition to a gallery of photographic portraits that half-filled the wall at the end of the *Herald*'s second-floor newsroom in an old Victorian block on Edensburg's Main Street. Founder Dan Osborne was there, and his son Tom, and a series of managing and news editors, one of the earliest scowling out from under a green eyeshade, several of the later ones sporting polka-dot bow ties above their bulging oxford-cloth collars—the entire gallery comprising what I later heard some of the younger *Herald* reporters refer to as "the dead white males."

Janet Osborne was the *Herald*'s first female editor, selected by her father upon his retirement in 1985 because, he told her, "You're the best man for the job." No one within the family, and few outside it, doubted the wisdom of the choice. Among Janet's siblings, only Eric had been as qualified as she was to put out the paper, and he hadn't been interested. He'd have had to come in out of the wilderness too often.

Eric's and Janet's brother Dan, namesake of the founder, had approximately the right politics for the editor's job, but he was notoriously hotheaded and inept in his interpersonal relations and would have driven the entire news staff at the *Herald* up the wall or out the door in a matter of weeks. Nobody in the family wanted that, despite the tug of Dan's name, pedigree, and gender. Nominally, Dan Osborne was "publisher" of the *Herald,* but a nonfamily member actually ran the business side of the paper, freeing Dan to organize on behalf of leftist third-party political candidates and lead sugar-harvest expeditions to Cuba.

Dan's early participation in the Venceremos Brigades was a source of sour amusement with the two of Tom Osborne's offspring who somehow turned out politically conservative. Chester, an Edensburg stockbroker, and June, who had devoted her years as head of the Eden County Museum board of directors to keeping twentieth-century art out of the museum and all but out of the county, regarded their siblings'— and parents' and grandparents'—unshakable principled liberalism as a family pathology. Some families produced a lot of harelips, others a lot of liberals.

Neither Chester nor June, however, had ever dared interfere with *Herald* editorial policy. For one thing, deference was due Osborne family tradition, however mushbrained Chester and June considered it. And anyway, the two weren't about to tangle with Janet and Dan—both scrappers who could get rough—or their widowed mother, Ruth Osborne. Even as her health had begun to falter, Ruth was understood by family members to be fully capable of protecting the *Herald*'s progressivism with savvy, diligence and—on rare, awful occasions—cold fury. Once, at a family picnic, June's husband, Dick Puderbaugh, chortled over a *Herald* editorial calling for Richard Nixon's impeachment— this was early in Nixon's *first* term—and Ruth tore into her son-in-law savagely, calling Nixon and Henry Kissinger war criminals who ought to be in United Nations–run prisons, and making a connection between the napalming of Asian babies and Dick Puderbaugh's fuel-oil dealership. This was a linkage that even young Dan, then a leader in the SDS, thought might be going too far.

Ruth's role in Osborne family affairs had been complicated recently by early signs of Alzheimer's disease, but only Janet knew about that. She did not expect her mother's so far negligible mental impairment to figure in the family battle over whether to sell the *Herald* to the good chain or the bad chain—the daisy chain or the chain of fools. But Janet was concerned enough over her mother's mental state that every day she stopped by the old Osborne family home on Maple Street after work en route to "the lake house," the Osborne summer home that Janet now shared year-round with her lover, Dale Kotlowicz.

I learned all of this Wednesday morning while sitting in Janet Osborne's office, a glass-enclosed rectangle overlooking the *Herald* newsroom. The desk and decor in Janet's editorial headquarters—which had been her father's and grandfather's—were late Victorian, but the old Underwood typewriter up on a shelf and the pneumatic tubes for shooting copy to the linotypists in the rear of the building had been replaced for practical purposes by a video terminal and computer keyboard. And alongside the old framed wall photos of earlier Osbornes posing with Teddy Roosevelt, Franklin and Eleanor (separately), Chester Bowles, and Al Gore Sr., among others, Janet was pictured smiling happily in the company of Audre Lorde and Adrienne Rich.

Janet gave Timmy and me her twenty-minute Osborne-and-*Herald*-family-and-newspaper history, explaining in the course of her narrative how it all led up to the current crisis. The paper had always been profitable, she said, but in 1988 Stuart Torkildson, the Herald Company's vice president and chief operating officer, came up with a plan to ensure the paper's future economic health in the face of rising costs and growing competition for ad revenues. The company would cash in on the Reagan go-go economic boom with an $18 million mountain resort twenty-six miles from Edensburg in the village of Blue Valley. Profits from the resort, to be called Spruce Haven, were meant to guarantee the paper's survival—and editorial independence, Stu Torkildson emphasized—for at least the next century.

Most of the Osbornes loathed the Republican president that one of the *Herald*'s 1986 editorials referred to as "an amiable blowfish," as they did "the country-club piranhas who swarmed in his wake." But the Spruce Haven design won prizes for both its esthetics and its uncompromising environmental sensitivity. And if cashing in on the Reagan boom could protect the paper's traditions against the general ongoing dumbing down of American journalism—now often combined with advertising and public relations in a watery porridge called "communications"—then it made sense to borrow the $16 million the family would need to see the project through and plunge boldly into the new millennium.

Tom Osborne, exhausted and near death from liver cancer, reluctantly endorsed Spruce Haven, as did Ruth, June, Chester, and even Dan. Janet and Eric voted no—they argued that the idea might be sound, but the size of the loan was too risky. And when the Reagan boom went bust, it turned out that Eric and Janet had been right. The customers didn't come—there was no theme park, no casino, no Frank, no Liza—and the resort consistently ran at a third of its capacity and lost money. The Boston bank that had loaned the Osbornes the $16 million got fed up with late or nonexistent mortgage payments and finally declared that if the family company refused to sell its assets—including the still-profitable *Herald*—then the bank would seize those assets and sell them to the highest bidder.

That's what had led to the family's decision to sell Spruce Haven for whatever amount they might squeeze out of it—a few million had been the broker's prediction, and it was accurate—and to sell the *Herald* to either (a) the highest bidder, no matter how sleazy the buyer or (b) the bidder most likely to keep the Osbornes running the paper or, failing that, likely to retain the large, excellent staff and maintain the paper's ever-fussy journalistic high standards and unreconstructedly liberal editorial page.

In early March, Crewes-InfoCom, whose reputation was for stripping newspapers and reducing them to little more than shoppers' guides, made an offer that would have left the Osbornes, after taxes, with roughly $8 million to divide. A week later, Harry Griscomb Newspapers, a Portland, Oregon, chain, offered several million less; in selling to Griscomb, the Osbornes would escape with only a few hundred thousand dollars after paying off the bank and the Internal Revenue Service. Harry Griscomb, however, saw the *Herald* as a treasure of American journalism whose traditions he vowed to uphold, and for several of the surviving Osbornes that promise was worth more than money. Several other offers fell in between InfoCom's and Griscomb's, all of them from chains whose journalistic standards ranged from the elastic to the unlocatable.

Janet, Dan, Ruth, and Eric planned to vote for selling the *Herald* to Harry Griscomb. June and Chester were for Crewes-Infocom. The deadline for bids had been August 1, with a sale deadline of September 10 imposed by the Spruce Haven mortgager, which was itself in trouble and itching for its money.

Then on May 15, Eric was killed, by a deranged drifter, police believed. In his will, Eric left his personal belongings and cash assets to his lover, Eldon McCaslin, with his share in the paper—which could be transferred only to another family member—going to his mother. But the company by-laws said no member of the board of directors got more than one vote, so after Eric's death the pro-good-chain margin dropped from 4 to 2 down to 3 to 2. If somehow Janet, Dan, or Ruth died or became too incapacitated to participate, the board would be split, and—with the by-laws requiring that the size of the board never fall below five members—a fifth member would be added to break the tie. The antiquated board rules stipulated that the new member must be the eldest offspring of the eldest third-generation Osborne. Eric and Janet had had no children; Janet and Dale were planning either to adopt a child or for Dale to bear one, but that hadn't happened yet. So if a new member were to come on to the *Herald*'s board of

21

directors, it would be June's attorney son, Titus—or "Tidy," as he was known around Edensburg. And, as his mother had made plain, he would vote to sell the paper to Crewes-InfoCom, the bad chain.

Therefore, Janet told us, it was critical to the *Edensburg Herald*'s future that she and Dan and Ruth Osborne survive at least until September 8—when the board of directors' vote was scheduled—with their hearts beating and their faculties intact.

4

He came tear-assing out of a cove about a mile up that way," Dale Kotlowicz said, gesturing dramatically, "and zoomed straight at Janet, as if he was some heat-seeking missile and Janet was an F-16's jet exhaust."

"When he was closing in, I heard him coming and took a quick look," Janet said, "and then dived deep, and when I surfaced he'd made a sharp U and was headed straight at me a second time. I waved like crazy—at first I figured the numbskull just wasn't paying attention— and when he just kept coming, I dived again, straight down and kicking hard, and I was saying to myself, 'Don't panic, don't panic, don't panic.' "

Janet was tall and rawboned, like all the Osbornes I'd seen in *Herald* photos, so it was hard to imagine a Jet Skier not noticing her big head and long arms, even at dusk, especially a second time. We were standing at the end of the wooden dock behind the Osborne lodge on Stilton Lake where Janet and Dale lived. Dale was smaller and probably ten years younger than Janet and was topped by what looked like ten or fifteen pounds of black-and-gray tight curls. And inasmuch as both Janet and Dale radiated alertness, strength, and blunt intelligence, it made sense that anyone daring to attack either of them could only hope to get away with it with the help of high-horsepower machinery.

"And then," Dale said, "the asshole turned around and came barrel-assing back a *third* time, and that's when I ran out from the porch and started screaming, 'You dumb son of a bitch! You dumb son of a bitch!' "

"But by then I'd gotten the picture," Janet said, "that either the guy was blind and couldn't see me or—what it actually looked like—his eyesight was perfect and he meant to run me over. So the third time I dived I took a deep breath first and just headed back for the dock underwater. I didn't come up until I saw these pilings on my right. And by then, Dale was down here yelling her head off and the guy had doubled back again and was gone, back around the bend."

Timmy said, "How far did you have to swim underwater?"

"She was sixty or eighty feet out, for chrissakes!" Dale said. "If that maniac had hit her, I don't know if I could have gotten out there in time to drag her back—assuming she hadn't been killed by the impact and gone straight to the bottom."

"I know the water here," Janet said, "and my lung capacity is probably better than the average forty-six-year-old's. But I'll tell you, I was damn shaky when I climbed out of the water that night. The thing is, the one time I caught a quick glimpse of the guy's face, he seemed to be looking right at me. And he didn't look confused; he looked mean and purposeful."

I said, "Had the sun set yet? Is it possible the setting sun was shining directly in his eyes and the look on his face that you saw was actually some combination of disorientation and fear?"

Dale gave me a "duh" look. "Donald, do you think the sun might have been jumping back and forth from one side of the lake to the other? The guy went after Janet *three times.*"

Janet said, "Anyway, the sun had already set. It was dusk with some red in it, and just a couple of low, dark clouds in the southwest. It's a perfect still time for an after-dinner swim, or a slow canoe ride. Once you get out a ways, you're only aware of the water around you and the sound of your own motion through it, and then as the light fades and the stars come out, the sky. It's always been my favorite time of day or night on the lake."

"The other nice thing about that time," Dale said, "is that you see fewer power boats after sunset, and hardly ever Jet Skis. It's the time of day when the owners of such devices tend to be enjoying their cocktails—which more often than not come in packs of six and are bound with thin strips of plastic."

Timmy said, "It's tempting to place a Freudian interpretation on men achieving a sense of power by *v-room-v-room*ing around a body of water with internal-combustion engines wedged between their legs."

"That's right," Dale said, "when the only thing most men need to do to achieve the same effect is to eat more beans, sit in their bathtubs, and blow it out their butts."

I said, "Janet told us you were a doctor, Dale. What are you, a gastroenterologist?"

"No, I'm a heart surgeon."

"Ah."

Timmy said, "Where do you practice, Dale? At Albany Med?"

"Yes, I'm on vacation for the month of August. The rest of the year I work seventy to ninety hours a week, but I do make it a point to stay up here all of August every year and rediscover nature and literature and my lover. So, what's the deal? Are you guys going to find out who's after Janet and protect her? Eldon said you were some kind of hot-shit private eye in Albany, Don."

Timmy said, "Yes, he is."

"Let's slow down for a minute," Janet said. "It does look as if someone tried to run me over with a Jet Ski. But that was over a week ago, and nobody has come after me since then. I've been wary and alert, but there haven't been any suspicious or threatening incidents at all. So the Jet Ski thing could have been a weird, isolated event with no explanation we'll ever have. Or is that wishful thinking?"

"What it is, is bullshit," Dale said.

Janet gave Dale an affectionate look, as if Dale had just uttered a familiar endearment, and said, "I admit that the Jet Ski scare coming on top of Eric's being killed makes me nervous. I'm just not sure, Don, what you or anybody else can do about it. The sheriff sent a deputy over, and he checked out the cove the skier came out of. There was no sign of the guy an hour later, and a couple of the people who live up that way said they did notice a skier that evening, but they didn't register where he'd come from, or where he went, or anything unusual about him. So going after the rampaging Jet Skier looks to me like a probable dead end."

I said, "What did the man on the Jet Ski look like? You said you saw his face."

"White, male, big, stocky, sandy hair pulled back, probably in a ponytail, broad face," Janet said. "I couldn't have gotten a close look at his face, but somehow I have it in my head that he looked cool and ferocious, as if he knew exactly what he was doing."

"That may sound like your typical outdoors internal-combustion overenthusiast," Dale said. "But this one was even worse than most. Homicide is a little much even for the crotch-rocket crowd."

We all peered out at the area of the lake where Janet apparently had been attacked. It was midafternoon—Janet had left the office early and we'd followed her the twelve miles out to the lodge—and the sun was still strong in a cloudless blue sky. On the far side of the lake, a mile or two away, I could make out several old wooden docks like the one we were on as well as newer, lower floating docks moored in front of the cabins and lodges that were back in the shadows of the pines. A cigarette boat buzzed up and down the far shore pulling a figure on water skis. Closer to our side, a lone man wearing a baseball cap paddled a canoe.

I said, "I'd like to talk to the deputy who came out last week, and to whoever investigated Eric's murder. Are they out of the same office?"

"You mean out of the same Cub Scout pack," Dale said.

"The deputy was Fulton Poorman," Janet said. "He's not terribly swift as a criminologist, but they sent him because he lives out this way. He's entirely approachable and actually a pretty nice guy. As for Eric's case, the sheriff, Ken Stone, doesn't have the resources, outer or inner, to handle a murder investigation. So he brought in the staties and they pretty much took over. See Captain Bill Stankie at the Edensburg barracks. He strikes me as competent, if unimaginative, but I'll be interested in getting your take on him. Dale thinks he's lazy, but I'm not sure about that. I think maybe he has his own tempo that he thinks is right for any particular investigation. And for Eric's case, apparently, it's a slow one."

Dale said, "Stankie's theory is it was a homicidal drifter—some twitchie dork by the name of Gordon Grubb who was in the area at the time and is now in jail down in Pennsylvania, where supposedly he shoved three campers off a cliff. Stankie's not trying to extradite him because there's no real evidence tying Grubb to Eric's death. Anyway, if he's convicted down there, the Commonwealth of Pennsylvania will no doubt want to send him spinning off to kingdom come expeditiously. My parents had a friend who went to Penn State in the forties, and she said whenever they threw the switch on 'Ol' Ben's Kite,' as they called it, at Rockview State Penitentiary, the lights dimmed up and down the Nittany Valley. Just your average inadvertent public execution."

Timmy said, "These days executions are so tasteful, and medically approved—lethal injections and all that."

"I don't believe there have been any 'medically approved' state executions in this country," Dale said. "Oh, in Texas maybe."

We were all sitting along the edge of the dock now. Janet and Dale had their sandals off, their feet dangling in the cool water.

Timmy said, "Why do you think Skeeter is so sure there's some connection between Eric's death and the Jet Ski incident and the situation at the *Herald*? He was acting pretty crazy at the hospital last night, but he seemed so certain about that—as if the drug that made him psychotic also heightened his powers of intuition."

Janet slumped a bit and looked rueful at this turn in the conversation. It was Dale who said, "Skeeter?"

"Eldon was called Skeeter when Timmy knew him in high school," Janet said, perking up at the chance to change the subject. "Where did his nickname come from anyway?" she asked Timmy.

"I don't know. He had it from when he was a little kid."

"The Eldon I know is hardly mosquitolike," Dale said. "He's more ursine. But I guess it would make some people nervous having a tot around nicknamed Grizzly."

"Eldon was big and already had hair on his chest even when I first met him in seventh grade," Timmy said. "He was in my gym class, and I think it might have been my first locker-room erotic response."

"Mine was similar," Dale said. "Renée Boulanger was a French exchange student. She didn't have hair on her chest, to the best of my recollection, but she had it under her arms down to her hipbones, and I still get weak in the knees at the thought of her. I wonder what old Renée is up to now."

Janet suddenly hopped up and said, "How about a swim? Aren't you two ready to cool off?"

We'd brought our bathing suits along, although Timmy had said earlier in the car: "I know at some point they're going to whip off all their clothes, dash through the trees, and plunge into the lake—I guess you can't call it 'buck naked.' And they're going to expect us to do the same. Believe me, this is going to happen. I have a feeling about Janet Osborne and about any woman she might choose to live beside a lake with."

I told him that if he was going to be involved in the investigation of a crime—which he still insisted he was—he'd have to quit being so prim. So he buttoned his lip on the subject of our skinny-dipping with lesbians, obviously a complex circumstance for him.

Now, as Janet began to speak eagerly of watery recreation, Timmy said, "I'm really enjoying just sitting here, even with so many people living around the lake."

"Stilton is big enough," Janet said, "to accommodate quite a crowd. Although if tranquility is what you're after, stay away from here on holiday weekends. It's Orlando-in-the-Adirondacks."

"She's referring to the Florida city specializing in industrial tourism," Dale said to Timmy and me, "not the Virginia Woolf novel."

Timmy said, "Oh, I see. Thank you."

"Have you read it?" Dale said.

"Orlando the city," Timmy asked, "or *Orlando* the novel?"

"The great novel."

"No, but I read *To the Lighthouse.* By the time I'd finished it, I was experiencing the actual physical sensation of having multiple personalities. Only the greatest literature can do that."

At this, Dale cracked an enigmatic little smile.

Not daring to look at Timmy, I gazed out across the lake. The cigarette boat across the way was still zooming around with a skier in tow—a young man in multicolored boxers, it looked like—and a man in a baseball cap still paddled his canoe along the shore a quarter of a mile away.

Timmy said, "Janet, you were going to tell us about Skeeter's suspicions surrounding Eric's murder and the Jet Ski attack, and how they could be connected to the *Herald*'s situation. Does Skeeter have particular people in mind—in your family or at one of the newspaper chains—who might actually try to change the outcome of the vote by murdering people on the board of directors? Murdering Eric or you or your mother or your brother Dan?"

Janet stood motionless, outlined against the sun, and said nothing for a long moment. Fit and rangy as a basketball pro in blue shorts and a lemon-yellow T-shirt, she was remarkably sturdy for a woman in early middle age, but now her fear made her seem vulnerable. She suddenly looked so anxious that I half expected her to dive off the dock and speed away in no particular direction.

Dale said, "Some of the newer Osbornes have a part or two missing. Or six or eight. The gene pool got spread thin or something."

Janet lowered herself to the dock again and sat beside Dale, who squeezed Janet's hand, then let go. Janet smiled weakly and said, "The

Osbornes have always advocated peace and love." She forced a laugh and added, "But they haven't always practiced it."

Dale said, "Present Osborne company excepted, of course."

"I have a temper too," Janet said. "You guys haven't seen it, but Dale can tell you."

Dale rolled her eyes. "I can, but I won't. Anyway, what we're talking about here is more than the odd hissy fit. It wasn't Janet who killed her brother. And Janet didn't get mad at herself and try to bash her own head in with a speeding Jet Ski last week. I know that because I was there."

I asked, "Do some Osbornes have a history of violence?"

As Dale watched her, Janet said to me, "Some do, yes." She took another breath and said, "My mother's brother Edmund once nearly beat a man to death with a walking stick. Uncle Edmund is dead now, but I mention this because there seems to be a pattern, a predisposition to violence among the Watsons, my mother's family. It's probably not genetic—the best science on the subject comes down against that possibility. But the tendency nevertheless is there. A therapist I once talked to about it called it image copying. That's where someone internalizes the image of a relative and consciously or unconsciously follows a kind of life script where she or he emulates a bad relative's bad behavior. There are several examples of it in my family. Among my generation, my cousin Graham, Edmund's son, has been in prison since 1992 for stabbing a man in a bar in Lake Placid and nearly killing him.

"Eric was never violent, and Dan's not, and I'm not—so far—and neither is June. We've all been known to yell and storm around, Dan especially. But the only one of the siblings who's shown any of the Watson tendencies is my brother Chester. When he was an adolescent, he lost it twice at hockey matches and bashed guys on the opposing team with his hockey stick. The second time he did it, he beat a boy so badly that Chester was charged with criminal assault. It was only his age and Slim Finn, Dad's lawyer and Edensburg's Mr. Fixit, that got Chester probation instead of juvenile detention. Chester hasn't hurt anybody since then, that any of us knows of, but Chester's son, Craig, is in prison too. Last year he shot and killed a guard in a jewel robbery."

Janet paused here to take another deep breath, and maybe to get a reaction. Timmy said, "So it's a kind of Watson-Osborne floating bad seed. Not genetic, but persistent nevertheless."

Dale gave Timmy a look and said, "That's certainly tactless."

Timmy stiffened—tact and discretion were among his strong points, he correctly believed. But Janet smiled reassuringly and said, "No, that's exactly what it is. I've used the same terminology. In fact, so has Dale. There does seem to be a kind of bad seed on the loose—at least metaphorically speaking—in the Watson-Osborne clan's psychological makeup."

"It's different when I use the term," Dale said. "I'm family."

Recklessly, Timmy opened his mouth again. "Are you two in a formal union?" he asked.

"Yes, the ILGWU," Dale said.

"No, our union has been blessed by neither church nor insurance company," Janet said. "But Dale's been around for eight years, and she's a family reality."

"Some of the Osbornes can even stand to be in the same room with me," Dale said.

"Eric and Dale adored each other," Janet said, "and Dan and Mom like her a lot. June and Chester don't have what it takes to appreciate Dale, I have to concede that."

Dale said, "One time somebody told us that when he's among his golfing buddies, June's husband, Dick Puderbaugh, refers to me as 'Janet's Jewess.' June once asked me if it was hard for me to adjust to living in the Adirondacks instead of the Catskills."

"This from the enlightened Osbornes," Janet said. "Some of the family's seeds are bad, and some apparently are just dumb and mean."

I said, "Who among the bad ones is pro Crewes-InfoCom to the point where he or she might try to change the outcome of the board vote next month by killing Eric or you or Dan or your mother?"

They all looked at me, and then we all looked at Janet. She had sat down again and had been absently kicking the surface of the water with her foot. But she stopped now and gave me a strained look. "I don't know," she said. "Chester? Conceivably. I'm never sure what's going on in his head. I can't quite make myself believe that Chester would hurt any of us. And yet I know how bitter he can be about those of us—especially Dan and me—who have kept up the *Herald*'s liberal traditions, which Chester despises. June has never been physically violent, and yet I know how badly she wants both the money from the sale of the paper and for the paper to fall into the hands of a chain whose reactionary politics are closer to her own.

"So who does that leave? Neither Chester's nor June's spouse has any history of physical violence. Nor do their kids—except for Chester's boy Craig, and he's been in prison for more than six months. Tidy, June's boy, seems to take out his minimal frustrations in bridge tournaments. And her other son, Tacker, went surfing in the South Pacific four years ago and hasn't been seen since. He sends Dick and June an Australian Hallmark card every Christmas and Easter. That's it. There's nobody left. So who could it be? Chester? Nobody? Is this some paranoid delusion I'm having? Or that Eldon's having? Of course, Eldon started in on this conspiracy-theory stuff before he went into the hospital and went psychotic. Almost from the first, he thought the timing of Eric's murder was cause for suspicion, and then, in Eldon's mind, the Jet Ski incident clinched it that something truly hideous was happening."

I said, "Have Dan and your mother reported any threatening incidents?"

Janet shook her head. "No, but I've wondered if I should talk to them about Eldon's suspicions. I don't want to freak anybody out—especially not Mom. Yet on the other hand, what if there really is some danger?"

"How much do you know about Crewes-InfoCom?" I asked. "Have you ever heard of them using strong-arm tactics, or worse, in order to pull off a deal where some of the owners of a paper were resistant to selling?"

"The company is known for 'playing hardball,' to use the eighties macho-man vernacular," Janet said. "But actual violence, no. There's no history of bludgeoning balky shareholders to death, that I know of, if that's what you mean. Talk about your hostile takeover."

Timmy piped up and said, "It sounds as if someone well-qualified does need to investigate this thing, though—either to expose and finish off any plot against you or your mother or your brother, or to reassure you that no such plot exists so you can relax and get on with the job of saving the *Herald*. Don't you agree, Janet?"

She hesitated for just an instant, then said, "I think so. It looks that way."

"Well . . ." Timmy began. His voice faltered suddenly, and he looked away, overcome with emotion. We waited, awkwardly, Janet and Dale looking surprised and concerned. Then Timmy cleared his throat and went on. "The thing of it is," he said with effort, "helping you and keeping you safe and saving the *Herald* are the main things Skeeter cares about right now. It's probably the main thing he wants to stay alive for. And because I care about Skeeter, and I, uh, owe him something, I think . . . I'd, uh . . . I'd like to finance the investigation. For Skeeter. And for you. And in Eric's memory."

We all looked at him and waited for someone else to react. Dale started to open her mouth, then apparently thought better of it.

Janet finally said, "Timmy, that's a generous and touching offer. And while I'd love to accept it—and I do accept and appreciate the sentiment behind it—I have to tell you that I believe this is an Osborne family matter that the Osbornes ought to take all the responsibility for, including financial. I'd never accept money from Eldon for this, and so I really can't accept any from you. And the Osbornes can handle it, believe me. As for a gift in Eric's memory, there's a fund in his name at the Wilderness Society and I'm sure they'd be extremely happy to hear from you. I'm sure that Eldon would be touched too by any donation to the society that you'd like to make."

Timmy looked disappointed and was about to speak, but Dale cut him off. "Wait a minute. Don, how much do you charge, anyway?"

"Four hundred a day, plus expenses, and a retainer of twelve hundred dollars is customary."

"That sounds reasonable if you're any good," Dale said. "But if this thing drags on, Janet could end up coughing up quite a wad. I want to contribute too, so let's go threesies. Janet pays a third, I pay a third, and, Timmy, you bring up the rear. Come on, Janet, we all want to help, so don't be such a hard-ass. Let us help out. I love you and I want that you should be well, and Timothy here wants to help because he's still carrying a torch of some kind for his old high-school hump buddy. Plus, the *Herald* is a good cause. Anyway, if you spread the expense three ways, and Mr. One-Man-Mod-Squad Strachey here doesn't produce, there'll be three of us to jump him and give his balls a good twist."

Janet looked uncertain but seemed to be mulling this over. Timmy glanced at my lap, then back at Dale. I said, "That sounds like a workable arrangement, Dale, for the most part."

Janet said, "The company is in no position to pay for this, and I've already taken two pay cuts. So I guess I'd better go along with this generous arrangement, at least for now. So, thanks. Believe me, I appreciate it."

We all looked at Timmy, who finally said, "Okay. But I want to help not just with money. I really want to be involved. I really need to be doing this. For Skeeter."

Ol' Hump-Buddy Skeeter.

An hour later, the four of us were fifty or sixty feet out in the lake. We were all wearing bathing suits. Almost simultaneously, we heard a deep buzzing noise that got louder and louder very fast—too fast. I heard Janet scream, "It's him! *Dive!*"

Timmy and Janet were about twenty feet farther out than Dale and I. I thought I heard a light *whomp* as I dived, and when I surfaced, about halfway back to the dock, Janet was nowhere in sight. But I saw Timmy and Dale come up and take a quick look around—the skier had made a U, spotted us, and was speeding back our way—and then Timmy and Dale gulped in air and dived again. I did the same. My heart was pounding and I was sick with fright for Janet as I swept through the murky lake water, but when I broke the surface again ten feet from the dock, Janet came up ahead of me, unhurt, and scrambled gasping up the ladder onto the dock. The Jet Skier was zooming away now, up the birch-lined shoreline. Timmy and Dale shot up like two whales dancing, though not so gracefully, and swam toward the dock—Timmy lagging behind a bit—where I joined them.

"It was that guy!" Janet yelled. "It was that same mean-eyed homicidal creep!"

I clambered onto the dock and hollered to Janet, "Let's go! Up the shore! In my car!"

We sprinted up past the lodge and jumped into my Mitsubishi. Janet directed me out the driveway and up the shore road. The clutch pedal was sharp under my bare left foot, and the gas pedal felt weightless and weird under my right. We could hear but not see the skier, and then Janet caught a glimpse of him through the trees, and she yelled, "He's cutting out across the lake! Shit, we'll never catch him now!"

I said, "Who lives over there? Anybody you know?" I did a quick, gravelly turnaround in somebody's driveway.

"The Stebiks! I'll call the Stebiks and tell them to see where the guy docks that thing."

Back at Janet's, she tore into the house, me at her heels. She leafed frantically through her address book, then punched in a number. She waited, pacing, peering out at the kitchen window, dripping lake water.

"Hell. No answer. They're not home."

"Do you know anybody else over there?"

"No. Not in that area. Shit."

We raced back outside and saw the maurauding Jet Ski disappear behind a long dock a good two miles on the far side of the lake. We picked out landmarks—a house with white dormers, a red outbuilding—for locating the dock where the Jet Ski landed.

I said, "Don't you have a power boat?"

Janet shook her head. "Don't let Dale hear you say that."

We headed back out toward the dock, where Dale yelled at us, "Hey, I could use a little assistance here!"

Timmy was still in the water, clinging to the ladder, shivering and grimacing with pain.

"The thing hit his foot," Dale said. "Apparently when he dived to get out of the way, the side of the Jet Ski hit his foot. I've been down to check, and it's intact, but I think it's broken."

Timmy gasped out, "That jerk!"

Dale and I hoisted him up onto the dock and helped him lie on a towel Janet had spread out. Janet said, "I'll call the ambulance."

Timmy said, "What for?"

"You're going to have to get this foot set and immobilized," Dale said, "if you ever hope to do the hokey-pokey again."

"That guy was actually trying to kill us!" Timmy blurted out. Under his sunburn, he looked pale and feverish and as vulnerable as I'd ever seen him. A wave rolled through me, and it occurred to me that one day Timmy would die.

Janet, slumped and gray-faced too, said, "I think that vicious jerk was trying to kill *one* of us. Me, obviously."

None of us contradicted her, and it was Dale a moment later who went inside to report the attack to the sheriff's office and to request an ambulance for Timmy.

Janet said, "I guess I'd better go talk to Dan fast—and to Mom."

Squatting by Timmy, my hand behind his wet head, I told Janet, yes, she should get to both of the pro-good-chain Osbornes—the sooner the better.

5

We followed the ambulance in two cars to the Eden County Hospital. By the time Timmy was wheeled into the ER, his right foot was the size and color of a small warthog, and the ambulance crew had him so drugged up against shock and pain that he had begun to babble.

He told the nurse, "I'd like to be in Skeeter's room."

I said, "Okay, but that's down in Albany, and you'll have to hop there on your right foot."

"What's your name?" a man with a clipboard yelled in Timmy's ear. "Timothy Callahan."

"Have you got any coverage?"

"I prefer to pay cash."

I said, "He has excellent insurance," and showed the man Timothy's New York State Assembly employee's health insurance card, which I had located easily in his wallet, the slender purse of a fiscal ascetic.

A physician showed up, groped around, ordered X rays, and told us in due course that Timothy's injury appeared to be a simple fracture. If the X rays confirmed that, the fracture would be set and Timmy would be shoved out the door with a fiberglass cast and a pair of crutches in a matter of hours. I asked, Didn't they want to keep him for a week or ten days? But they said no. I told Timmy I'd be back to collect him later and left him with a copy of *Guns and Ammo* that I'd found in the waiting room.

I rejoined Janet and Dale in the parking lot, and rode in Janet's car to her brother Dan's apartment in a building next to the Eden House, the old Victorian hotel in the center of town. Dan Osborne and his girlfriend, Arlene Thurber, lived on the second floor in what had been two apartments. They had knocked down a wall to create a long, high-ceilinged salon with six windows overlooking Edensburg's Main Street and enough shelf space to hold their sizeable collection of leftist political history and analysis, from Bukharin to Fanon to Carlos Fuentes. There were lots of posters and photos too of Che and Fidel and a recent selection of Zapatistas wearing masks, but no Erich Honecker or Mengistu Haile Mariam that I was able to make out.

When we arrived, Dan and Arlene were just about to leave to drive down to Skidmore College in Saratoga Springs to see that evening's double feature in a Godard series, *Alphaville* and *Les Carbiniers*. Dan and Arlene seemed happy to have Janet and Dale show up, and they tried to persuade us to join them at the movies—until Janet told them why we had come by unannounced.

"It looks as if somebody is after me," Janet said. "And I guess it stands to reason that they might try to get at you too, Dan. I think you're going to have to be on your guard."

When Dan and Arlene looked more bewildered than alarmed, Dale spelled it out. "Not 'after' her, not 'get at.' What Janet means is, somebody is trying to *kill* her. And if the whole thing has anything to do with you-know-what, they might try to kill you too, Dan. Arlene, you're probably safe, theoretically, since you haven't got a vote on the *Herald*'s board of directors. But since you two are joined at the hip, Arlene, you could conceivably suffer what the Pentagon likes to refer to as collateral damage—that is, end up just as dead as Dan."

Dan was tall and gangly, like all the Osbornes, and he slumped a little when he heard this. He had a Fidel-style beard that was honey colored with some gray in it, making him look less like Castro than Gerry Mulligan, and his wide mouth dropped open beneath it. Arlene, busty, braless, and languid in purples and reds and Navajo silver, stiffened and exclaimed, "Dale, what kind of crazy shit are you laying on us? Are you serious?"

"Last week, somebody tried to run Janet over with a Jet Ski," Dale said, "and today he came back and tried to bash her again. There were four of us out in the lake this time, and Don's boyfriend, Timothy, got whacked on the foot. He's over at County right now having it set."

"That is too much!" Arlene said angrily.

"This happened just now?" Dan asked, looking dazed. His surprise was understandable, although his mind may also have been mildly fuddled by marijuana. Its weedy aroma hung in the room, a sweet cloud of sixties déjà vu for me and—judging from the numerous tiny roaches in the ashtrays—a routine nineties air freshener for Dan and Arlene.

"It happened about an hour ago," Janet said, "and the sheriff's department is supposedly trying to track the guy down. I'm alerting you two, for what it might be worth, and I really think I have to tell Mom because—well, you know. First Eric is killed and then this, and—it does seem possible that somebody is trying to change the outcome of the board vote on InfoCom and Griscomb."

Dan glanced at me uneasily—as if to say, This is private family business, and who is this bozo, anyway?—and then snapped at Janet: "Why am I just *now* hearing about this?"

"Because," she shot back, "it just now *happened,* Dan. That's why we're *here.*"

"But Dale said it happened *last week* too. I know nothing *about* that."

"Well, now you know, Dan. As I said, that's why we're here. That's why we *came* here. To *tell* you about it. Now the question is, What do we tell Mom?"

"What makes you think," he said, his beard flapping, "that this has anything to do with the sale of the paper? Where did you get *that* idea?"

"I don't *know* that there's a connection," Janet said in a sneering tone I hadn't heard her use before she had come into the presence of her brother. "I am merely surmising it from the rather startling sequence of events over the past three months. The paper is put up for sale and two conflicting offers are made, putting the family at one another's throats. Then Eric is killed. Then two attempts are made on my life. I'm just adding two and two together and coming up with four. When you add two and two, what do *you* come up with, Dan?"

Making a show of struggling for control, Dan took a deep breath and said, "Yes, the timing *is* suspicious, Janet. That I can see. What I'm having a lot of trouble accepting is that InfoCom would go so far as to actually try to kill an Osborne. God, imagine how it would make them look if they were caught. Does the sheriff have any leads? Who's investigating this, Ken Stone?"

"It's Ken," Janet said, "but it looks as if the attacker got away both times. He's obviously someone who knows the homes on the lake."

Arlene looked suddenly horrified and said, "It's like Karen

Silkwood! Dan, we'd better make sure your mother is safe. Crewes-InfoCom would off an old lady if they thought she was going to interfere with their bottom line. They'll stop at nothing to protect their corporate profits."

Dan didn't react to this. He just peered our way with his watery blue eyes. It seemed now as if they were no longer focused entirely on those of us in the room, nor was the mind behind them. Finally Dan said to Janet, "Tell me again what happened, and why you think these episodes were deliberate attempts to—to attack you. This Jet Ski run-over-attempt thing actually happened twice?"

Dale nodded slowly and held up two fingers, and Janet described once again the attack the previous week and the attack a few hours earlier that had landed Timmy in the emergency room.

"Now, who's this Timmy again?" Arlene said.

Dale said, "He's Don here's boyfriend. Don is a private investigator from Albany who we're hiring to clear everything up, including Eric's murder. We're giving him about four days to produce results."

"You're a private eye with a boyfriend? How cool," Arlene said. "Are you bisexual?"

Before I could reply, Dan said without hesitation, "I'm not sure that's such a great idea. I mean bringing in someone from outside."

This was addressed to Janet and I let her answer it. "Why is it such a terrible idea? The police have made no progress at all toward solving Eric's murder. And if somebody is trying to kill me too, there's at least a good chance that the same person is behind it—or people. But convincing Ken Stone of that, or even the staties, is going to be tough with no real evidence to go on. And Don has an excellent reputation, according to Eldon, who's an old friend of Don's boyfriend."

"How's Eldon doing?" Arlene asked.

"I'm sure Don's C.V. is impressive," Dan said to Janet, dismissing my résumé with a little wave. "But that's not my point. My point is, by bringing in someone who's outside the paper and outside the family at this sensitive juncture—someone who's going to take months just to gather background—you run the risk of having him going around stirring up people's suspicions and exacerbating an already tense situation without gaining anything positive. If there is some kind of plot against you or me or even Mom, we can hire a security service to protect us. If anybody asks why, we can just say Eric's murder freaked us out, and having protection for a while makes us feel more secure. Don," Dan said, looking me in the eye for the first time since we'd been introduced, "are you associated with a firm that does security work? If you and your firm could confine your work to guaranteeing the safety of Janet and myself and our mother for a month or so, that could be extremely useful to our family, and I think we might be able to do business."

I was about to reiterate to Dan that I had already been hired by Janet, Dale, and Timmy to conduct a full investigation of Eric's death as well as the two Jet Ski attacks on Janet, and that Dan's view of the matter was interesting but of peripheral concern to me. Before I could, Janet, her face red and her neck muscles taut, laid into her brother.

"Dan, if you'd quit being some kind of Osborne patronizing twit for one minute," she sputtered, "you'd think about what this apparent attempt to kill me really *means*. It probably means that Eric wasn't killed by a homicidal drifter but by someone in our family. Don't you get that? It's probably not InfoCom that's behind this at all. I mean, how many corporations, no matter how cold-blooded and greedy they are, actually put out contracts on people who get in the way of their expansion opportunities? Let's face it—what this is is probably more Osborne violent craziness. I have no idea who in the family might be doing it, and to tell you the truth, I'm trying hard not to think about it. But a skilled outsider is exactly what we *do* need at this point. Not a shopping mall guard, but an experienced investigator. I've done some asking around about Don, and he comes extremely well recommended. And Dale and Timmy and I are hiring him, whatever the hell you think. So get used to it."

Dan looked everywhere in the room except at his older sister as she told him, in effect, that he was a pompous man who struck silly poses, and his opinions were dumb and irrelevant. When she had finished, he reddened, but said only, "Do I actually have any goddamned *choice* in the matter?" It looked like the reenactment of an old familiar scene in Osborne sibling annals.

Arlene tried to help. "Kerr-McGhee put out a contract on Karen Silkwood, Janet. And what about Inslaw?"

By now, Dan looked so cowed and miserable—his sister's light was obviously hot and bright in his life—that I was happy to lessen the tension in the room marginally by acknowledging Arlene's existence, which seemed to slip Dan's mind when he was in the presence of his sister, and by reminding Janet that there was an aspect of the situation she seemed to have analyzed carelessly.

I said, "I think Arlene might be right, Janet, not to rule out corporate involvement in any kind of conspiracy. If there is a murder plot, that would be unique among assaults perpetrated by Osbornes, not characteristic. The examples of Osborne violence you described to me were spontaneous outbursts, never premeditated—as far as anybody knows—and not conspiratorial. The victims were all nonfamily members. Which is not to say that one or more family members might not be conniving this time—with or without the participation of InfoCom. But there's no evidence yet pointing to any Osborne—or, for that matter, anybody else. For an investigator, the family and InfoCom are simply logical places to start."

Janet eyed me stolidly and didn't react. Dan had listened to my assessment with what looked like mounting apprehension as it dawned on him, apparently, that my digging into Osborne family conflicts might be both intelligent and dogged.

It was Arlene, though, who said, "I'm just glad somebody is finally going to do a real investigation of Eric's murder. I'm not saying the cops were covering up. But they sure haven't done much beside sit on their fat asses. So good for you guys and Don's boyfriend for hiring Don to do the cops' job. Are you taking contributions? I'd like to help out if there's a fund."

"See me afterward," Dale said. "Your generosity is appreciated, Arlene."

"I'm also going to be sending Don lots of good energy."

Janet said, "Look, I don't want to prejudge anybody, either, but what's happening to the Osborne family now, and to the *Herald,* is not a soccer game or a barroom argument or some juvenile criminal escapade. Just about everything is at stake for the Osbornes this time— the family business, the family name, the family history, for chrissakes. So it's possible that the particulars of past Osborne extreme behavior might be an inadequate guide."

"God," Arlene said, "all the Osbornes are tantrumy, and June and Chester and their kids are all reactionary pigs. But the idea that somebody in the family that we all know might actually get in bed with a corporation and murder a relative, even if they hate their guts—that just makes me want to puke!"

Arlene seemed to be speaking figuratively, but Dan looked suddenly queasy and bolted from the room. He pulled the bathroom door shut after him, but not tightly, and we could hear him retching.

6

That's June's car," Janet said irritably. "What could she be doing here?"

We had pulled into the driveway of the old Osborne house on Maple Street. The place was one of those grand old late-Victorian relics with a wraparound porch, turrets, and bow windows. The house obviously had been built back when coal, lumber, and Irish servants were plentiful and cheap, and when Americans aspired to large, prosperous families full of large, healthy people. Most of these big houses in Edensburg, as elsewhere, had long since been divided into more economical rental units, but Ruth Osborne had hung on to all of hers. The shade was inviting under the immense maples, and the well-tended clumps of larkspur, delphinium, bee balm, and coreopsis between the main house and the carriage house were as showy and robust as the age when the garden must have been first planted.

Back by the carriage house, three cars were parked ahead of Janet's, the one we arrived in.

"June wouldn't have heard anything yet, would she?" Dale said. "I don't think she consorts with either criminal riffraff or law-enforcement riffraff. At least, not that I know of."

As we got out, the side door of the house opened and a man and a woman walked down the steps. "Oh, shit," Janet said. "I hope they weren't interrogating Mom."

The two figures who approached us were a large woman in a mauve silk dress and a dough-faced man with an odd, S-shaped mouth and a straw boater on his head. I assumed they were Janet's sister, June, and her husband, Dick Puderbaugh, but I was only half right.

"Hi, June, Hi, Parson," Janet said. "What brings you two around Maple Street?"

"Janet, hi, hi," June crooned, and squeezed Janet's hand and Dale's elbow. "Dale, Dale, it's awfully nice to see you too." She looked like an Osborne, big and open-faced and handsome, but with a tightness in her manner that was accentuated by a snood on the back of her head that suggested not so much provincial respectability as cerebral strangulation.

"Well, if it isn't the *Herald*'s esteemed editor in chief!" the man in the boater hooted in a nasal baritone. He had on white slacks and a seersucker jacket, like a member of a barbershop quartet, and behind his spectacles he had a twinkle in one gray eye. The other eye looked appalled.

Janet handled the introductions all around, naming me but not my occupation. June watched me suspiciously, and Parson Bates, the man in the straw hat, grinned smarmily and said, "Donald, may I be so bold as to inquire if you are—as you appear to be—a New York-uh?"

"Be so bold, Parson," Dale said, but Bates ignored her.

"I live in Albany," I said, "which I'm afraid is where people usually say I appear to be from."

"Oh, that other big city!" June said, her eyes bugging out in genial mock alarm.

"Are you up our way to take the waters?" Bates said, chortling.

"But there are no waters here," Dale said. "This is the desert."

Janet said, "Donald is working for me for a period of time. He's in Edensburg in a professional capacity, Parson."

"Oh, yet another wretched scrivener!" Bates sputtered gaily out of one side of his mouth, and his twinkly eye twinkled and his other eye maintained its gorgonlike stare.

"Don's a private investigator," Janet said, and we all watched June's face change expression a dozen times in fast forward.

Bates said, "Gadzooks!"

"It has to do with Eric's murder," Janet said. "And another situation that's come up."

"What on Earth is that?" June said.

"Attempts on my life."

"Oh, Janet, no!" June clutched her head carefully.

Janet described the Jet Ski attacks of the previous week and of that afternoon, not mentioning anyone's suspicions that the attacks might be connected to the conflict over future ownership of the *Herald*.

"I would venture to opine," Bates said, "that such a matter might properly fall within the province of law enforcement. Would it not?"

"The sheriff's department has been notified," Janet said. "I take it, June, that no one has come after you or threatened you recently."

"Me? Lord, no! Why in heaven's name would anyone?"

"Indeed!" Bates said, in high dudgeon at the very idea.

"Well, Eric was killed and now it looks as if somebody is trying to kill me. Maybe somebody has it out for some of the Osbornes—I don't know. That's why I've hired Don. To find out."

Dale said, "Actually, three of us hired Don to investigate Eric's murder and the Jet Ski attacks. Janet is one of the three, I'm another, and the third client of Don's is his own boyfriend, Timothy Callahan, who's an old boyfriend of Eldon McCaslin. In fact, Timothy was injured in the incident at the lake today, and he's over at Eden County right now having a broken foot set."

June stared at me, working hard but not hard enough to keep from looking queasy, and said nonsensically, "How nice."

Parson Bates's look had darkened, and he started to speak but then appeared to think better of it, and his mouth clamped shut.

"We're going to have to lay this all out for Mom," Janet said, "as much as I dread upsetting her. How is she today?"

"Oh, she's—Mom," June said, affecting nonchalance, although her snood constricted perceptibly. "Now, has Chester been notified about your hiring an investigator?" June asked.

"No, not yet."

"Chester will want to know."

"Why don't you go ahead and fill him in, June? I've already spoken to Dan and Arlene. We're just coming from their place."

"Oh, I'll be glad to. And of course Dick. Frankly, Janet, I'm surprised none of us was consulted before you hired an investigator to start rummaging around in the family's affairs." She gave me a chilly smile. "I'm sure you're extremely well qualified, Mr. Strachey, don't get me wrong. But, do you understand what I'm saying?"

I said, "No, I don't."

June flinched, and Bates gallantly stepped forward to deal with this damnable insolence. "June was referring to the fact and the idea of discretion," Bates harrumphed. "It is a virtue that is rapidly disappearing from American life, where, thanks to the dominance of a vulgar and conscienceless electronic media, just about every citizen's bedroom and toilet habits are fodder for open and casual discourse. There are those persons, however, who bravely resist this social and moral degradation. June Osborne, I can state without fear of contradiction, is one of those good persons."

June looked apprehensive over Bates's confrontational style, if not, I guessed, his sentiments. Janet and Dale both peered at me poker-faced and waited.

I said, "You've missed the point, Parson. Number one, I'm not Diane Sawyer or Larry King. I'm a private—let me emphasize private—investigator. The results of my inquiries are seen only by my clients, two of whom in this case are members of the Osborne family." June looked as if she didn't like the sound of that, and Bates, picking up on my reference to Dale as an Osborne, glowered theatrically.

"Secondly," I went on, "I'm interested in peering into Osborne family bedrooms and toilets—your linkage, not mine, Mr. Bates—only insofar as either might shed light on Eric's murder and the recent attacks on Janet. A more general rattling of family skeletons is not what I'm aiming at. Doing that would be—yes, I wholeheartedly agree—rude and indiscreet." June's look softened a bit, but Bates, apparently anticipating a trap, still gave me the fish eye.

I said, "But the question I want to ask you, June, is this: Why do you believe my investigating your brother Eric's murder and these apparent attempts on Janet's life would necessarily lead me into Osborne family affairs?"

"Oh," she said, and then had to think about this. "I didn't mean to say that you'd be probing into the entire family's affairs. Just Eric's and Janet's."

"But Eric is dead and Janet is my client, so what's the problem?"

June just stared at me, but Bates came to her rescue again in what seemed to be the only way he knew: He perspired energetically in his seersucker jacket—the temperature had to be in the mid-eighties—and he puffed himself up and fumed. "Osborne family matters are intertwined," Bates declared. "An investigation into the affairs of any one Osborne necessarily will impinge upon the business of other family members for whom discretion may be valued highly. The situation is not nearly so simple as you are making it out to be, Mr. Strachey. It is complex and demands attention to the opinions of others."

Dale said, "What do you mean the 'business' of other family members, Parson?"

"I don't catch your drift."

"You said an investigation into the affairs of any one Osborne necessarily will impinge upon the 'business' of other family members. By business, do you mean the *Herald*?"

"Not the *Herald* in particular," Bates sniffed. "Have you drawn that inference? Be assured, no such implication was intended."

Janet said, "The thing of it is, Parson, that with Eric dead and if I were dead, it's almost certain that the *Herald* would be sold to Crewes-InfoCom and not Griscomb. So anybody investigating Eric's murder and attempts on my life would naturally want to look into the family business and its current turmoil. Catch my drift?"

Now June bridled. "Janet, what do you mean by that?"

"I mean that the people with a motive to see me and Eric dead are the people who want to sell the *Herald* to InfoCom and the people at InfoCom who want to buy the paper. If you were the investigator and you were considering motives to murder Eric and me, isn't that what you would look at first?"

"But, my lord, Janet! Can you seriously consider that someone in the family would ever do such a thing?" June looked aghast as she said this, and then something seemed to hit her, and she looked aghast a second time.

"For chrissakes, June, the family tree is ripe with violent nut cases," Janet said. "Would you like me to recite them for you?"

"That won't be necessary. But the people you're talking about now, Janet—the family members you evidently regard as under suspicion of murder—these people are not troubled individuals like Cousin Graham or Uncle Edmund or even Craig. You can only be referring to . . . to me and to Dick and to Chester and . . . and to Tidy! Janet, how could you even think such a thing!"

Dale said, "June, chill out. Janet is just explaining why Don might have to do some sniffing around in the Osborne dirty laundry. Don't forget that under our system of criminal justice, you and Dick are innocent until proven guilty. Of course, if you decide to retain a crackerjack criminal lawyer, that's up to you."

June bit her lip, but Bates could no longer contain his indignation. "Dale, your infernal flippancy is . . . out of place!"

"I thought it was perfectly placed myself. It's the Osbornes trying to save the soul of the *Herald* who are getting knocked off, not the Osbornes who are willing to sell out a hundred years of great journalism in order to turn a quick profit. My flippancy pales next to their greed."

June's eyes flashed with anger. "Dale, you certainly are trying everyone's patience today," she said, edging toward her Buick. "And I think Parson and I had better be on our way before one of us says something he or she later regrets. And Janet, I do believe you would be wise to take your family murder plot ideas and run them by Stu Torkildson before you go to the police and start a lot of talk that can only do untold damage to the entire family. Try to be a little farsighted, will you? Or," June said, with a look of fresh alarm, "have you already gone blabbing outside the family?"

"Not yet," Janet said.

"Good. Mr. Strachey, I guess we'll all have to depend on your discretion, like Parson says. Why don't you arrange to have a talk with Stu Torkildson too? He's the Osbornes' business adviser of many years, and when it comes to sensitive situations, Stu is a rock."

"He could look up, for example," Dale said to me, "if anybody in the family has signed a recent contract with Murder, Inc."

I said, "Isn't Torkildson the man who came up with the investment idea that forced the *Herald* into such deep debt that you're now forced to sell the paper? You mean he's still around?"

Dale gave me a look that said, "Now you're catching on," and Janet watched us all benignly.

It was Parson Bates who blurted out, "Your gall, Mr. Strachey, is exceeded only by the depth of your misinformation. The *Herald*'s financial difficulties were caused not by poor judgment, but by changing circumstances no one could have foreseen. Not even Stu Torkildson, a man of keen mind and Christian probity, could have predicted a recession and a one-hundred-twenty-five percent increase in newsprint costs. I take strong exception to your maligning this man of character."

I said, "I thought the company's sixteen-million-dollar debt was the result of a risky, grandiose resort project that didn't pan out and had to be sold at a huge loss. I wasn't suggesting that Torkildson was wicked, just vainglorious and dumb."

"Yes, that's the conventional wisdom on the *Herald*'s troubles," Bates said. "But the truth of the matter is a good deal more complex, I can assure you."

"Clue me in on the complexities. I'm all ears."

Bates was about to speak when June cut him off. "Perhaps we could rehash the *Herald*'s troubles another time, Mr. Strachey, but not just now. Parson and I really must be on our way. It was a pleasure to meet you, and it was nice to see you too, Dale. Janet, keep me posted on this awful Jet Ski business. I do hope it's not what you seem to think it is. Losing Eric was horrible enough, and none of us in the family wants you to be run over and drowned, Janet, no matter what you might think of us. And, of course, another murder would just kill Mom." At this, June let loose with a hysterical giggle, and yelped, "Oh, what in heaven's name am I saying!"

"Well, what *are* you saying?" Dale asked, but June had turned in confusion and was climbing into her car.

"Good luck!" June sang out wackily, and Bates lowered himself into June's Buick beside her, sniffing and throwing eye darts at us, like in the funnies. The car eased around us and cruised out into Maple Street and away.

After we watched the car go, Janet said dryly, "Don, you probably think June's looniness is atypical among the Osbornes."

I said, "No, don't forget that I've met your brother too."

"Right."

"Who's the reverend?"

"He's not a reverend. Parson Bates is his name. He's a local pear farmer, antique spats dealer, and the neo-con columnist for the *Herald*. Dad always believed that in a one-newspaper town like Edensburg the paper had a responsibility to give opposing voices a forum, provided that their bigotry is at least thinly veiled, which Parson's generally is."

Dale added, "Both Parson's politics and his moral beliefs are barely distinguishable from Cotton Mather's, although he sees himself as marginally more modern than that. He does, however, draw a line at the twentieth century—which he disapproves of more or less in toto—and he styles himself as a kind of genial nineteenth-century, belovedly dotty country squire. Parson does have a devoted following—not including, of course, those *Herald* readers who suspect that he may be clinically insane. In his columns, Parson likes to draw lessons to live by from nature. And when he's out in his orchard and the raptures are upon him, and he starts hearing his pears offering moral instruction, look out. His 'unnatural' personal and social evils range from Wal-Mart to welfare to gangsta rap—which in one column he insisted on referring to repeatedly as 'gangster' rap. And, hey, don't get Parson started on cunnilingus."

I said, "He actually deals in old spats? Not petty-argument spats, but those cloth-and-leather things people used to wear over their insteps and ankles?"

"Parson is world renowned among spats collectors," Janet said.

Dale added, "People come from all over, every year, by the ones and twos."

"Not all his bêtes noires sound unreasonable to me," I said. "As a social evil, Wal-Mart would be high up on my list too."

"Parson is actually an interesting mixture," Janet said, "of small-is-beautiful and small-minded-is-beautiful."

"And he and June are chums?"

"Since seventh grade. June and Dick and Parson and his wife, Evangeline, play whist out at the Bateses' every Friday night, and they're all on the board of the museum together."

I said, "Has Bates ever been known to turn violent?"

"Not physically," Janet said. "Anyway, I know he's ambivalent about the *Herald*'s being sold to InfoCom. He's loyal to June and he'd love to see the paper's liberal traditions interred, but he also hates ruthless, amoral big business. So it's hard to imagine Parson involved in a plot to do away with me or Dan or Mom. On the other hand, it's also true that Parson and Eric couldn't stand each other."

"They fought?"

"Avoided each other, mainly. Eric had no patience with the way Parson used nature in his writing to support his prejudices, including a raging homophobia that's just barely under wraps. And Parson was jealous, I think, of Eric's talent and success as a nature writer. Also, Eric's and Eldon's being casually out as a couple drove Parson gaga. He was always fuming to people about them—an affront to nature, and all that. Dale and me he tolerates more easily. First of all, we're women, and not to be taken so seriously as men. Also, I think, he sees us as a 'Boston marriage,' one of those nineteenth-century eccentric institutions even the religious Emersonians made room for in their expansive universe. But two men together? The horror, the horror."

Dale was about to add something to this when the side door of the Osborne house opened again, and a stout, middle-aged woman in powder-blue slacks and a peach-colored blouse came out and, looking distressed, called Janet's name.

"Elsie, hi, we'll be right in. How's Mom?"

"Not good. You'll see as soon as you get in here. She's not good."

"What's the matter?" Janet said, looking alarmed.

"It's her mind," Elsie said, tapping the side of her head with her finger. We followed Janet quickly into the big house.

7

The woman seated in a bay-window breakfast nook just off the kitchen looked up at us and smiled uncertainly but did not get up. In her early eighties, Ruth Osborne was still tall and sturdy looking—"statuesque" in the parlance of her young adulthood—with sun-bronzed rough hands and a long face with large curious eyes, as in a painting of a Bloomsbury figure. She had a big head of Gravel Gertie hair and wore a shapeless green shift. Lying alongside, but not on, her bare feet were a pair of worn leather sandals.

"Hi, Mom," Janet said, and kissed her mother on the cheek. "How are you doing? Dale and I brought a friend along."

Mrs. Osborne looked at Dale without apparent recognition and then at me. As Mrs. Osborne studied me, Dale leaned down, kissed her on the cheek, and said, "Hi, Ruth," but the old woman stiffened and looked embarrassed.

"I'm Don Strachey," I said, and Mrs. Osborne extended her hand, which I grasped. Her skin was dry, her grip firm.

Without enthusiasm, she said, "I always enjoy meeting my daughter's friends."

"Don's up from Albany," Janet said. "He's a private investigator down there."

She took this in, smiling tentatively, and said, "Oh, that's nice." Then she turned and looked out the window. We followed her gaze and all of us peered out at the backyard, where the sun shone down on the freshly mowed lawn and beyond the trees there were shadows.

"Mrs. Osborne, that's Dale there," Elsie said. Janet had introduced Elsie Fletcher to me on the way in as her mother's longtime housekeeper. She said, "You know Dale, don't you? That's Dale there." But Mrs. Osborne did not respond and continued gazing into the backyard.

"I'm the mouthy one," Dale said. Then Dale looked at me. "Ruth and I always hit it off," she said, "on account of we're both—as people around Edensburg like to call it—'outspoken.' If we hadn't seen eye to eye on so many things, we'd probably have strangled each other."

I said lamely, "I'll bet."

Ruth Osborne was now somewhere else, and when Janet said, "Mom?" she got no response.

"We'll be back in a few minutes, Mom," Janet said, and indicated for us to follow her.

Dale, Elsie, and I went with Janet down a dim, wide hallway and into a book-lined study, where Janet shut the door. The oak library table in the center of the room was heaped with books, as was the old leather swivel chair behind it. It looked as if some sorting out of Tom Osborne's library had commenced some years earlier but had not gotten far. The oil portrait over the fireplace of a man in a turn-of-the-century man-of-parts getup appeared to be the *Herald*'s founder, Daniel Lincoln Osborne. Below the painting, faded family photographs were propped on the mantel, with Tom, Ruth, and the five children at different ages and in various poses, most of them in wilderness settings. Also on the mantel was a bronze urn with a lid on it. An inscription had been typed on a sliver of paper and taped to the urn. It read: WILLIAM T. "TOM" OSBORNE—1911–1989.

Janet said to Elsie, "How long has she been like this?"

"Since yesterday morning," Elsie said, looking frightened. "I was going to call you today if she didn't snap out of it. June called this morning and said she'd be stopping in, but I was going to call you anyway." Elsie and Janet exchanged significant looks.

"And she was like this just now when June was here?" Janet asked. When Elsie nodded, Janet said, "Oh, God." To me, Janet said, "For a couple of years now there's been short-term memory loss, and she's gone blank on occasion—just sort of zombied out for five- and ten-minute periods. But nothing this long lasting."

"Mrs. Osborne was always a talker," Elsie said. "She had a mind like a whip, and boy oh boy did she ever let you know exactly what she

54

was thinking. That's not Ruth Osborne out there, what you're seeing now. Not by a long shot."

Dale said to me, " 'Be prepared,' we were told as children. But what can anybody do to prepare for this?"

"What did June want, anyway?" Janet asked."

"We go weeks without seeing June," Elsie said to me, clearly hopeful that I might become an ally in her disapproval of a daughter who didn't visit her mother often enough. To Janet, she said, "June and Parson both wanted to talk about selling the *Herald* to that big company that sounds like somebody sneezing."

"InfoCom?"

"Yes, they wanted Mrs. Osborne to vote for that one."

"Parson too?"

"Both of them did, yes. They tried to get Mrs. Osborne to come in here with them and shut the door, I suppose. But she wouldn't budge from the breakfast nook, so I heard a lot of what was discussed. I had baked corn to get in the oven, you know."

Janet picked up the cue and said, "Mom sure loves your baked corn, Elsie."

"Oh yes, she enjoys it when I cook."

"So what did Mom say about InfoCom and her vote?"

"Why, she didn't say anything at all. She said hello and how do you do and not a word more, as far as I'm aware. Several times while they were here, June said, 'Mom, what's the matter?' Or, 'Mom, are you listening to me?' She knew your mother wasn't right, Janet. She saw that it was more than just forgetfulness this time."

"Did June say anything about it to you?"

"No, but she gave me a look on the way out—like I knew all the time your mother's mind was going, and now June knew it too. Parson Bates was all smiles, but he was right there the whole time, so he got the picture too, you can bet your boots on that."

"I ran into them on their way out," Janet said, "but neither one of them mentioned anything about Mom's being different."

"Those two are up to something," Elsie said ominously, and no one in the room contradicted her.

Janet told Elsie she would contact Mrs. Osborne's physician, who had diagnosed early stages of Alzheimer's disease a year earlier, and find out if anything should or could be done at this point. Dale said that was wise, but in her medical opinion little could be done with Mrs. Osborne beyond help, patience, and kindliness. Experiments were underway with drugs, but so far the benefits were far from certain.

We were about to leave the study when the door suddenly opened and there stood Ruth Osborne smiling in at us. "I was wondering where you all had got to," she said pleasantly. "It looks as if you must have gone looking for something to read."

"Mom, hi!"

Dale said, "We weren't reading, Ruth, just visiting the family museum."

"Well, this is certainly it. I'm Ruth Osborne," she said to me, extending her hand. She looked fully alert.

"Don Strachey. I'm honored to meet you."

"My husband could never part with a book, and neither can I. It's just acquisitiveness and a minor variety of greed. What good's a book if it's not passed around and read? All these books being held captive here—for what? It's one of my six or eight moral weaknesses."

I said, "You always think you're going to reread them."

"Oh, not me. I have no illusions about that. I just like knowing they're in here gathering dust. The only ones I look at anymore are my son's books. Eric was a marvelous writer. Have you read him?"

"My lover and I sometimes read Eric aloud to each other when we're in the mountains. It's like having a companion with us who has a sixth sense for understanding the wilderness and who can put it into English."

"Yes, he was extremely gifted. Eric was murdered in May, however."

"I know. I'm sorry."

Elsie eased out the door of the study and threw an astonished look back at us as she went.

Mrs. Osborne said, "The police say it was some mysterious drifter who did it, but I wonder. The Osbornes have been a progressive force in these parts for a good, long time, and it wouldn't surprise me if somebody decided to get even with me or my husband by murdering Eric. Tom's dead, of course—that's him on the mantel—but Janet and my son Daniel and I are carrying on the family's progressive traditions, and some of the reactionary forces we've taken on over the years are ruthless people with long memories. And I've got another theory too that's even uglier than that one."

"Mom," Janet said, "Don is a private investigator, as a matter of fact. He's going to be looking into Eric's murder. He's also investigating something else that's come up. I don't want you to worry, because I can take care of myself, but—well, the thing is, somebody may be trying to get at me too."

Mrs. Osborne's brow furrowed and she said, "I'm not surprised to hear it."

"You're not?"

"No, not with the vote approaching on the sale of the *Herald*. With you or Dan or me out of the way, the vote would shift from a majority for Griscomb to a majority for InfoCom. Millions of dollars are at stake, and, of course, control over the soul of the paper. Bloody murder has been committed over a lot less. I've thought about warning you, Janet. But when you're my age you hesitate to tell people—even family, or *especially* family—that you suspect plots. People are liable to think you're losing your marbles."

Janet blushed. "Oh, Mom, you know you can always talk to me and Dale about anything."

I said, "Was there anything in particular, Mrs. Osborne, that set off your suspicions of a plot?"

Janet gave me a quick glance that I took to mean it might not be wise to encourage her mother's imaginings. But Mrs. Osborne said somberly, "Yes, it first hit me that something might be afoot about a month after Eric's death when Janet's older brother Chester came by and tried to persuade me to change my vote to support selling the *Herald* to InfoCom. Chester threw a fit—he's always had a vicious temper, which I'm sorry to say comes to him by way of the Watsons, my family—and he whooped and hollered about the family losing so much money in a sale to Griscomb that in order to keep that from happening, somebody else might have to get hurt."

We stared at Mrs. Osborne, who looked at us miserably. Dale said, "Somebody else?"

"That's what Chester said. 'Somebody else might have to get hurt.' "

"Mom, for chrissakes, why didn't you tell me this?"

"Janet—does this make any sense? I think I forgot. I know I meant to tell you right away. But . . . crazy as this sounds, I think I just forgot to."

The phone next to me rang, but no one in the room moved to pick it up and I heard Elsie answer it in the kitchen.

I said, "Mrs. Osborne, did you ask Chester what he meant by his threat?"

"No," she said, "I was so mad at Chester, I just told him to pick up his bundle of papers and to get out of my sight. Which he did. Mad I was, and a little bit frightened of him too. It's a terrible thing for a mother to think about, but I know from painful experience that Chester can hurt people."

"Did you think he was threatening you?" Janet said.

Mrs. Osborne shrugged and looked profoundly sad. Elsie had appeared beside her, and now she said to me, "Mr. Strachey?"

"Yes?"

"There's a man on the phone for you. I think it's important."

"A man by the name of Callahan?"

"Yes. Mr. Callahan. He sounded tetchy."

"That's because he broke his foot, and the hospital has probably finished with him and is about to shove him out to the curb in a wheelchair and leave him there. Maybe one of you could wait here," I said to Janet and Dale, "and one of you could drive me over to rescue Timmy."

"Sure, let's go," Dale said. "The ER staff won't abandon him at the curb, but they'll park him in a corridor somewhere and treat him like a misplaced cadaver on a gurney. He won't like it."

"And then," I said, "I'd like to track down Chester and ask him some questions. Is he in town?"

"Yes, and probably out at the club by now," Mrs. Osborne said, checking what looked like a huge Timex on her wrist. "But it wouldn't be a good idea to go interrogating him there. You could probably catch him at home after seven. He and Pauline generally watch the CNN business report over drinks at seven and sit down to dinner at eight. Are you going to question June too, Mr. Strachey? That's my other daughter. She doesn't have the history of violence that Chester does, but she's a treacherous piece of work in her own right."

We all looked at her. "I'm sure I'll be talking to June too," I said.

"Good. Be careful of them both."

"Okay."

"I haven't seen June in weeks," Mrs. Osborne said, "but I'm sure she's out there somewhere conniving to destroy the wonderful institution that was built by her grandfather and her father. That's my husband right there on the mantel," she said, "in that urn that could stand a good polishing. Tom was a remarkable man, and I miss him with such hurt. Maybe I'm nuts—it runs in the family—but I like to come in here and sit by that urn once in a while, especially in the evening. And believe it or not, it helps. Tom had requested that his ashes be scattered over the mountains, and Eric and Janet were shocked when I refused to let them do it. But I happen to draw comfort from Tom's gravelly presence up there. And he's not in any position to mind, so what's the beef?

"Of course, I wanted to stash Eric up there too, beside his father. But Eldon was sure Eric would want to be left out in the woods where he was happiest, so I acquiesced. Oh, it's all so hard and complicated. Mr. Strachey, don't outlive the people you love—that's my advice. It's just way too hard. I want to live until September eighth, when I can vote to save the *Herald,* but after that—well, we'll see."

"Mom, what do you mean!"

Mrs. Osborne let out a mordant little laugh. "Oh, don't get excited, Janet, I'm not about to pull a plastic bag over my head, and of course I'd never own a gun. I'm just talking."

In the awkward silence that followed, I could just barely make out the distant sound of a man's raised voice coming out of the telephone receiver down the hall in the kitchen. I couldn't pick up his words, just his plaintive tone.

8

I think I might be revising my position on capital punishment," Timmy said. He was in the front passenger seat of Janet's car, which Dale was driving, heading back to the Osborne house. I was behind him massaging his neck. He smelled of lake water and sweat and the fiberglass cast on his broken foot.

"What has your position been on capital punishment?" Dale asked.

"Against it. It morally demeans the state that carries it out, it has no demonstrable deterrent effect, and since the justice system is imperfect, it's inevitable that innocent people will be executed. But that asshole on the Jet Ski could have killed me, and now I'm mad."

"If he was tied down," Dale said, "and you were there with a Tongalese pigsticker, would you slice his guts open?"

Turning, Timmy couldn't get around quite far enough to catch my eye. But I caught his meaning: What is *with* this woman? Instead, he said, "I was speaking rhetorically."

"Oh. Oh, I see," Dale said blithely.

I had told Timmy about the visit to Dan and Arlene's, and Dan's vomitous reaction to our speculation that an Osborne might be plotting to murder—or to have murdered—another Osborne over the *Herald*'s sale to a good chain or a bad chain. I also filled him in on our unsettling encounter with June Puderbaugh and Parson Bates, and on Ruth Osborne's thirty-hour lapse into insensibility and subsequent recovery.

"Of course," Timmy said, "I'm doing my level best trying to keep some kind of rational perspective on this whole frightening business. I realize that my injury was inadvertent—a line-of-fire unlucky accident. And a broken foot is paltry next to murder. And it certainly does sound

61

from what you've discovered just in the past couple of hours, Don, that any number of people in this whole rat's nest that you've uncovered are capable of murder."

Dale said, "Are you saying, Timothy, that to you the Osbornes are a family of rodents? That seems rather sweeping."

I saw the blood rise in the back of his neck as he snapped, "Dale, you seem to have some kind of hair across your ass in regard to me. Why is that?"

By shifting a little, I could see her face in the rearview mirror. Her eyes narrowed and she said, "I do believe you're imagining that, Timothy."

"Hey, do you think I have some vital parts missing, or what? I am not imagining that no matter what I say to you, you are sneering and sarcastic, and you talk like I'm some kind of half-wit. Which I am not. Now, what exactly is the problem?"

For a long moment she just watched the road and drove, and said nothing. Then she said coolly: "You really don't remember me, do you, Timothy?"

"No, Dale, I am not aware that we were ever acquainted."

"Well, you should be aware."

"Oh," he said, "let me think. What could it have been? Now, did we sleep together once in the seventies? Were you ever a man?"

She made a face that said, "Oh, please."

"If you think," Timmy said, "that I'm the one who gave you anal herpes, be assured that you are mistaken. I've never had it."

"He's right about that, Dale," I said.

She looked for a brief instant as if she might crack a smile, but her control was sure and none appeared. She said, "I want you to think about it, Timothy. It was not a friendly encounter. If you think hard, it will come back to you."

"Oh, we're going to play games now. Swell."

She said, " 'Swell.' There's a word you rarely hear anymore. 'Swell' goes a long way back. That it's currently most often used sarcastically, as you used it just now, only adds to the word's quaint perdurability."

I had resumed massaging his neck and paused now to check the pulse behind his right ear. It was up.

I said, "Maybe, Dale, since we're all going to be spending a good bit of time together on a matter of current great importance, it would be best to clear the air on this other matter. Don't you think?"

She said nothing as she turned off Main and onto Maple Street.

"After all, you and Janet and Timmy and I are financial partners in this investigation," I said. "Based on long experience, I can tell you that when clients squabble, trouble ensues in an investigation. My professional advice is to get this business out into the open and see if you can't get it behind the both of you."

Dale pulled into the Osborne driveway and parked alongside a big patch of bright blue delphiniums that looked like the Emerald City. She turned to Timmy and enunciated the words, "April—1987."

He looked at her, mystified and clearly irked. "I haven't the faintest idea what you're talking about," he said. "Perhaps you're confusing me with Ronald Reagan. Did you ever have a run-in with Ronald Reagan in 1987? I'd love to have been a fly on the wall at that encounter."

"You're not too far off," Dale said, and got out of the car and strode into the house.

9

Just after nine, I pulled into Chester Osborne's cul-de-sac on Summit Hill Road, a woodsy residential drive on a high hill overlooking Edensburg. The light was nearly gone from the murky sky, but it hadn't cooled off much and the August night air was only a little less dense than gumbo.

I had my car back, and Janet and Timmy had driven down to Albany to visit Skeeter and pick up some of Timmy's and my belongings so that we could all move into Ruth Osborne's house together for a time. Our purpose was mutual protection. Dale would be there too, and she had agreed to quit sniping at Timmy for the duration of my investigation. She did insist that a "shoot-out" at some convenient later date was inevitable. Timmy told me he was almost convinced Dale was batty, but he conceded that something about her was starting to become very dimly familiar.

Chester and Pauline Osborne lived in a two-story mock-Tudor house built on a shelf of fill on the downslope side of Summit Hill Road. The house looked freshly painted and stuccoed, and the height of the arbor vitae rising out of the bark-mulch beds that bordered all the walls of the place suggested it had been put up in the early eighties. The cul-de-sac had been newly tarmacked and was brilliantly floodlit. His-and-her Lexuses were parked in the driveway, one glistening black, one glistening teal.

When I had phoned earlier, Chester said he was disturbed to hear that Janet had felt the need to hire a private detective—June had undoubtedly been on the horn pronto following our late-afternoon encounter. Chester told me he was interested in hearing about my "unnecessary" investigation, and why didn't I drop by for drinks after dinner? My own dinner, a couple of burritos, had been consumed at a picnic table outside Taco Bell. And while I wasn't sure which after-dinner drink was going to be appropriate, I had more pressing matters to take up with Chester Osborne, the stockbroker older brother with the history of violent outbursts.

"You found your way up here," Osborne said in a businesslike way. "Good for you. Well done."

"I followed your directions," I said. "They were clear."

"There's nothing worse than vague directions," he said with such finality that I decided not to bring up Chechnya. Leading me across the foyer, Osborne said, "We'll go in the study."

He was tall and stiff-backed in a gray pinstriped suit and silk tie with tiny blue digital clocks on it. Pleasantly large-featured in the by-then-familiar Osborne way, he carried himself with an assurance that suggested Janet's self-possession. Although something in Osborne's cool, blue, mildly bloodshot eyes hinted at a turbulent interior more like Dan's. Whether June's wackiness would also show up in the mix, I couldn't tell yet.

"Make yourself comfortable," Osborne said, indicating a striped-silk wing chair that looked as if it had been designed for anything but comfort. "Brandy?"

In some of the venues my line of work had taken me into, "Brandy," was more likely to be the name of a transvestite I was questioning than a beverage being served, and in that respect Chester Osborne's study represented a notable change. I said, "Yes, please."

The study, like the foyer we'd come through and the living room I'd briefly glimpsed (the back of a woman's blond head had been visible above the back of a couch), had wall-to-wall gray carpeting and the kind of furnishings more commonly found in investment bankers' offices: shiny formal chairs upholstered in silk or leather, heavily lacquered wooden sideboards, and desks whose design was vaguely, but not exactly, French provincial—more French Provincial Decorating Product. The watercolor of a mountain lake with a canoe on it hanging over Osborne's desk was identical to the watercolor of a mountain lake with a canoe on it hanging in the foyer.

"Looks good," I said, accepting a snifter half full of an amber fluid of considerable clarity. "No need to run this stuff through cheesecloth."

Ignoring that, Osborne stared at me for a long moment, and then said, "I spoke to my sister June earlier."

"I supposed you might have."

"June told me she ran into you today."

"Yes, this afternoon, at your mother's house." I sipped some of the brandy, which was not Fine Brandy Product, but the genuine article.

"June is a bit of a dingbat," Osborne said gravely, "but don't get the idea that I am."

"Okay."

He gave me an appraising look that was not friendly. Then he said, "I didn't like that talk about murder. June said you and Janet and Dale Kotlowicz were speculating about my brother's murder and what might have been an attempt to kill Janet—some crap about a Jet Ski attack. June doesn't always get her facts straight, but she reported to me that there was talk connecting these incidents to divisions within the Osborne family over the sale of the *Herald*. I didn't like that."

I said, "It was a theory that came up."

"Well, I don't like it. It's too close to slander." Osborne gazed down at me with his bloodshot eyes. He was still standing beside the bar a few feet from me, holding a snifter that he had not drunk from.

I said, "Any questions of slander could keep a couple of law firms' meters running indefinitely, but I'm more interested in finding facts, Chester. The police think a drifter killed your brother, and I'll be looking into that shortly. There is some evidence that somebody is trying to kill Janet, and with millions of dollars hanging on her vote on the *Herald*'s sale, any prudent investigator is going to consider a connection. Of course, as an experienced investigator, I know enough to keep an open mind and I'll follow any trail of evidence wherever it may lead. Do you have any idea, Chester, why anyone might want to kill Janet?"

He stared down at me, still holding, but not drinking, his brandy. "No. I don't," he said. "You'll have to ask Janet about that. Or Dale Kotlowicz."

"Why Dale?"

"Dale and Janet are dykes—husband and husband. You didn't pick up on that?"

"Oh, sure."

"They have their private lives, which I know very little about and which I try not to think about. If someone is trying to kill either one of them, that's what I would look at, the lesbian angle. What I would not do is, I would not go poking into the Osborne family's business affairs, if I were you. You won't learn anything useful in your investigation, and you're liable to make some people mad who are people it would be better for you *not* to get mad."

"You, for example?"

"Me, for example."

Violent history or no violent history, what a twit he was. I said, "What are you, some kind of small-bore mobster, Chester, and you're threatening to smash my liver with a tire iron? Or do you talk like that because you spend too much time watching old Louis Calhern pictures on the Nostalgia Channel? Either way, I'm unimpressed."

He flushed and glared hard, and it occurred to me that Osborne was going to fling his drink in my face. But he maintained control—I had a feeling he devoted much of his energy in life to maintaining his emotional and physical equilibrium—and after a moment of what looked like bitter reflection, Osborne said, "And I'm unimpressed with you, Strachey. You think you've got me pegged as some small-town, country-club blowhard, but your impression is too limited to do you any good, and I'm not going to correct it. That's because, for one thing, I'm not given to psychobabble. For another thing, who or what I am is none of your goddamned business. And for a third and very important thing, you've got a lot of gall coming into my house and insinuating that I would kill anybody, let alone my own brother or sister. It's not an accusation I feel I need to dignify with a response. Now, I asked you up here for a briefing on this investigation you're supposedly conducting, and you agreed to fill me in, so let's stick to that. It's possible, but not likely, that someday you'll be experienced enough in life and wise enough in the ways of the world to understand my background as Tom Osborne's son. But in the meantime, I would be very careful about any assumptions you make about me, if I were you."

He was still hovering over me with a brandy snifter in his hand, and this was making me nervous. I said, "Chester, I think you're right that maybe we've gotten off on the wrong foot here. Sit down and let me bring you up to speed on the investigation—which I can tell you has only just begun, and there's not a whole lot to tell. I especially don't want you to think I came here to threaten you. And I don't recall insinuating that you ever killed anybody or ever gave a thought to homicide. But do understand, your threatening me is a poor way to either gain my cooperation or affect the way I approach the Osborne family's personal or business activities. Your threats, as a matter of fact, serve mainly to pique my interest."

Osborne took this in with a show of fierce concentration, looking as if I were speaking in Esperanto and he was trying to follow somebody's simultaneous translation. Then he seemed to decide something, and he relaxed. He lowered himself into a wing chair, threw back the glass, and swallowed a slug of his brandy.

He said, "I don't like you, and I don't like what you're doing, Strachey. But I also know that refusing to cooperate with you is not the way to go. We'll just get each other riled up that way. I'm better off staying in touch, keeping tabs on you. So, with that in mind, I've set up a meeting for you tomorrow at nine-thirty with Stu Torkildson. You're to come by the *Herald* office. I'll also be present."

"I'll be there."

"Stu will reassure you as to any suspicions you may have regarding a connection between Eric's death and the sale of the *Herald,* or any connection between the sale of the paper and this ridiculous Jet Ski business. You need to be set straight on that score, and Stu can do it."

"How can he?" I asked.

Osborne looked nettled. "How can he what?"

"How can he reassure me that there's no connection between the sale of the paper and these other events unless he knows who killed Eric and why, and who tried to run over Janet with a Jet Ski and why?"

Osborne snorted once and looked at me as if I were a pathetic dunce. "You've never met Stu Torkildson, have you?" he said.

"Not yet."

"Stu is a persuasive man."

"So I've heard. But I hadn't heard he was all-seeing, all-knowing. Torkildson certainly lacked clairvoyance on the Spruce Haven resort project. After that bust—which is finishing off one of the more distinguished chapters in American journalism—I'm surprised you take this guy's judgments seriously at all."

Osborne dismissed this with a little wave of his brandy glass. "The financial loss is potentially considerable, but the rest of it, my friend, is just history. There's no point in getting sentimental over it. As a means of dispersing information, newspapers are all but dead. Half the people in the country own personal computers, and half of those are on-line. In another thirty years, newspapers will have disappeared, with books and magazines soon to follow old-time journalism into oblivion. By the middle of the next century, print on paper will be regarded as quaint, the way we look at gas lamps and phonograph records.

"The *Herald*'s days are numbered, no matter what happened with the Spruce Haven investment, and the only smart thing to do now is for the family to sell to the highest bidder, then take the money and invest it in something with a future. If Janet, Dan, and Mother had a head for business, they'd see that. But they're stuck in the past. They like the word 'progressive' and that's how they think of themselves. But, believe me, they are anything but progressive. Strachey, the only violence associated with the sale of the *Edensburg Herald* is the potential that eight million dollars will be flushed down the toilet. And if you want to prevent a disaster, my friend, that is the one you should be trying to put a stop to."

He gazed at me with his cool, bloodshot eyes and waited.

I said, "In June, a month after Eric died, you told your mother, Chester, that in order to keep the *Herald* from being sold to Harry Griscomb, the more responsible newspaper chain but the lower bidder—and here I quote you, Chester—'Somebody else might have to get hurt.' What did you mean by that?"

He missed just a fraction of a beat before he said icily, "I said no such thing."

"Your mother says you did."

A slight trembling of the brandy snifter and an emphatic shake of the head. "No."

"You seemed to be saying that you knew that Eric's death was connected with the sale of the paper, and someone else might die if that would ensure a sale to InfoCom instead of Griscomb. Your mother told me that your remark was unmistakably a threat."

His eyes flashed for an instant, but his fight for self-control was constant and, with me so far, availing. He said, "Then my mother did not know what she was saying. She talks gibberish half the time. If you were in her house today, you know that my mother is mentally ill. She is suffering from severe Alzheimer's disease. In fact, soon she may have to be institutionalized."

What was this? "Institutionalized?"

"Yes," he said, "Mother is mentally incompetent. I know it, and if you were with her today for any length of time, then you know it too. It's tragic to see this happening to a woman who always took pride in her intellect. June told me how heartbreaking it was this afternoon to find Mother sitting like a zombie and staring into her garden. What Mother needs now is professional care. There's just no getting around it."

"That's your opinion," I said. "Have you discussed it with Janet or Dan? Or with your mother?"

"Not yet," Chester said in a matter-of-fact way. "But June and I talked it over, and I called Franklin Whately, mother's physician. Frank was negligent in not filling me in sooner on Mother's condition, but this evening he brought me up to speed. So it's not too late to see to it that Mother is placed in the appropriate setting for someone in her medical condition."

"You called a doctor when you heard about your mother's supposed poor condition—which, incidentally, is not nearly so dire as you're making it out to be, Chester. And did you call a lawyer too?"

He hadn't smiled once since I'd entered his house, but now he came perilously close to betraying what must have passed for amusement with him. Osborne's face relaxed just perceptibly and he said, "What do you mean, did I call a lawyer? It would have been wildly irresponsible of me not to."

10

Janet said, "I'd almost be in favor of stashing Mom somewhere until the day of the vote if I didn't think Chester and June would pull some legal stunt declaring her incompetent in absentia, or some damn thing, and therefore ineligible to serve on the board and vote."

"It does sound like a trap," Dale said. "As if hiding Ruth is exactly what Chester and June want us to try. Otherwise, why would they tip their hand to Don tonight? Why not surprise us all and just show up one day when Ruth's home alone with Elsie and wave a piece of paper, clap her in irons, and haul her off until the vote is over?"

It was just past midnight and the four of us were having a beer on the screened-in back porch at the Osborne house. Three of us were seated on chairs by candlelight, and the place was quiet except for the hum of the air conditioner in the window of Ruth Osborne's bedroom up above us. Timmy was draped along a chaise, his fiberglassed foot shining in the flickering light.

"The other thing," Timmy said, "is that maybe everybody on the board who's planning to vote to sell the *Herald* to the good chain and not the bad chain is safe now, and there won't be any more murder attempts. Even if neither Chester nor June is involved in a murder plot, word will get around that they have a shot at neutralizing Mrs. Osborne legally, so anybody who'd planned on killing Janet, Dan, or Mrs. Osborne might be willing to adopt a wait-and-see attitude."

"Oh yes," Dale said. "We could take a chance and let our guard down. What have we got to lose but another human being?"

Timmy muttered something indecipherable, and I said, "I thought we had an agreement, Dale."

"Whoops."

Janet said, "I think Dale is right that since both the future of the *Herald* and people's lives are at stake, we have to hope for the best but plan for the worst."

"That's an extremely generous interpretation of Dale's remarks," Timmy said, and in the dim light I glared at him. He caught this, and added, "But I believe both of you are entirely correct in your estimation that continued caution is in order."

"What I'm going to do," Janet said, "is talk to Slim Finn in the morning. He was Dad's lawyer and he's Mom's. I'm sure Chester's got somebody else intriguing away, probably his golfing partner, Morton Bond, and Slim will know how to get a mental competency hearing postponed for the five weeks we need until the board meets, or—failing a postponement—have the hearing held on a day when Mom is compos mentis. Meanwhile, I guess at least one of us needs to be here with her at all times. Whenever possible, two of us."

We all looked at each other, aware of which two of us would be most often available over the next week for a watch over Ruth Osborne. I said, "This job is critically important," and Timmy and Dale both gave me an indignant look that said, There's no need to treat us like children.

"I'm also going to get Mom's physician, Frank Whately, over here," Janet said, "to get an updated evaluation of her Alzheimer's, and the best short-term prognosis he can come up with. God, I just hate it that Mom is facing this horrible thing—and I'm facing this horrible thing with Mom—at exactly the same time all this other putrid crap is happening with the paper, and Eric being killed, and the Jet Ski attacks, and Eldon being in the hospital. It's just—it's too damned much."

We all agreed that it was, but we sat there helplessly, making vague, useless, sympathetic noises. It was Janet who finally said, "At least Eldon is recovering from the pneumocystis, and he's no longer psychotic now that he's off the prednisone. There's that good news anyway."

"He was a little groggy when we saw him tonight," Timmy said. "And I got the impression he didn't remember anything he said to us last night. I mean, none of that nasty stuff about . . . what happened after high school. But he wasn't wild-eyed and crazy, and he did remember who I was, of course, and that I was there last night."

I said, "Of course."

Dale said, "Did either of you ask Eldon if he had any idea why Dan puked up his supper when he heard that there might be a connection between the sale of the *Herald* and Eric's murder?"

"Why would Skeeter know anything about that?" Timmy asked.

"Because he and Eric were sleeping together. Presumably they conversed about important matters."

Janet said, "Dan was completely devastated by Eric's death. I mean, we all were, and are—I still wake up in the night weeping when I dream about him. But at the time, it was Dan who really fell apart. And obviously he still hasn't recovered."

"Were Dan and Eric especially close?" I asked.

"In a messy, complicated way, they were," Janet said. "They'd been rivals for Dad's approval from the time they were toddlers. Of course, they were pretty much wasting their time in that department—Dad was not what you'd call warmly demonstrative with any of us. He saved his good opinions for the *Herald*'s editorial page, and his emotions too. But Dan and Eric both loved Dad and they both became journalists because of him. That was a bond between them. But then, because they were so temperamentally different—Dan being more Watson-like in his passions and volatility—they often fought, with Dan starting the fights and Eric, who was always stronger and more sure of himself, finishing them. Believe me, it was a busy, complex household to grow up in. As most households with big families are, of course. And households with small families too."

I said, "When you say, Janet, that Dan and Eric fought, do you mean physically?"

"Until they were both well into their teens. It's a big joke in Edensburg that this house full of pacifists used to erupt about once a week with crashing and banging and yelling, as if bloody murder was being committed inside." She caught herself, and when no one spoke, she added, "Please—don't even think it. Not Dan." More awkward silence. "It wouldn't make any sense," Janet said. "It just wouldn't. And I wouldn't be able to stand it."

After a moment, Timmy said, "It wouldn't make any sense, Janet, unless Eric's death and the Jet Ski attacks weren't even connected. And Eric's murder and the sale of the *Herald* had nothing to do with each other."

They all looked at me as if I, being a detective, might have an observation to offer that could clear the air a little, break the tension. But I didn't.

11

Thursday morning, Timmy, exhausted, slept in—we'd shared a frilly four-poster in what had been June's room—while Janet drove off to the *Herald,* Dale joined Elsie the housekeeper in keeping an eye on Ruth Osborne, and I left Maple Street at 7:45 in search of Captain Bill Stankie.

I drove out to the edge of town and found Stankie in his office at the State Police barracks, one of those characterless brick boxes that are representative of public architecture in the age of hate-all-government. Stankie didn't look as if he minded the lack of columns and a cupola framing his official presence. Squat, ruddy-faced, and agreeably unprepossessing in shirtsleeves and green suspenders, Stankie looked up at me placidly from behind his metal desk. I introduced myself and explained that I'd been hired by Janet Osborne to investigate any connection between her brother's murder and two apparent attempts on her life. For the moment, I left out the sale of the *Herald,* that day's edition of which lay open to the sports section on Stankie's desk next to his coffee mug.

"I doubt there's any connection, but I'd be interested to hear what you've come up with," Stankie said. "Have a seat."

I seated myself across from Stankie and told him that I was only just getting started and had come up with nothing of substance yet, and that was why I'd come to see him. I asked him to fill me in on the Eric Osborne murder investigation, and on anything Stankie knew about the sheriff's office investigation of the two Jet Ski attacks on Janet.

"Was that your boyfriend that got clipped yesterday?" Stankie asked. "My wife is a nurse at the ER, and she said a gay couple came in, and one of the guys had a broken foot from a Jet Ski incident out at Osborne's place on the lake."

"How did she know we were a couple?"

"Sue always knows. Our third son, Hank, is gay, and he and his partner, Ray, are both police officers in Cincinnati, Ohio—Ray's hometown. We don't see nearly as much of them as we'd like. We get out there once a year, but Hank and Ray are kept pretty busy with their off-duty gay-rights work. Cincinnati is a pretty conservative town. Which is fine with me, overall. I'm conservative myself."

"Except in one way, it looks like."

"Oh no," Stankie said with a shrug. "If you mean gay rights, that's conservative as I see it. The government leaving decent, law-abiding people alone is conservative. People being treated fairly is conservative. No, I don't see that I'm being inconsistent at all. It's the Newt Gingrichs that are being inconsistent." He paused, then added, "Not that I always saw it that way, I have to admit. I had to be educated on the subject."

"That's often the way it is. Although a lot of men your age are uneducable."

"I had no choice in the matter," Stankie said mildly. "It was come around or lose a son. So I came around. And it didn't take long, either."

"Then you had no problem with Eric Osborne's being gay. Or Janet's."

"Not in later years," he said, and I didn't probe into what that might have meant.

I said, "And when Eric was killed, you didn't immediately peg his male lover as the prime suspect, the way a lot of investigators might have."

"No, I knew Eric and Eldon well enough to see that their marriage was as good as mine is. But you shouldn't knock homicide investigators who take a close look at the spouse or lover first. Straight or gay, when a bed partner is murdered, often it's the other partner who did it. The statistics bear this out. In any case," Stankie said, looking a little embarrassed, "Eldon McCaslin had an alibi. When Eric was killed, Eldon was on a special assignment up near Watertown with two other forest rangers. Checking that out, of course, was a matter of routine."

"Of course."

"And anyway, on the second day of the investigation we started hearing about this Gordon Grubb character. Janet's filled you in on him, I take it?"

"She told me that he exists and you think he's the killer."

Stankie hesitated no more than a second, and said, "He's my candidate, yes."

"How come?"

Stankie pulled a folder from a stack on the side of his desk and extracted a rap sheet, photo attached, of a blank-eyed, thirty-seven-year-old man with a dirty beard and a jagged scar on his left cheek. "This is one of sixteen people who were known to have been, or could have been, on the trail Eric was hiking on the morning of the day he was killed. The other fifteen were upstanding citizens who had no connection with Eric that we could establish, or that any of them would admit to. Grubb had no known connection with Eric, either. But you'll see there that he's had two earlier arrests, including one conviction, for assaulting and robbing campers near Saranac Lake.

"A general store manager up where the hiking trail crosses Route 418 used to live in Saranac, and he recognized Grubb when he'd come into the store a day or two earlier. Later, other people who'd been on the trail that week picked Grubb's mug shot out of a series, and they said they'd seen him and he'd made people nervous on account of his looks. A week later, Grubb turned up in Tioga County, Pennsylvania, where he allegedly savagely assaulted and robbed three campers while they slept, shoving their bodies in a ravine. Two of the three died in the attack—they were all stabbed repeatedly with a hunting knife. But one survived, and he ID'd Grubb, who'd already been arrested in the next county for breaking into a vacation cabin. I drove down there and interviewed Grubb, but by then a lawyer had been at him. He refused to talk about anything at all, other than that he'd been up this way camping—he said he couldn't remember when. But is he our man on the Eric Osborne homicide? I'd say yes."

He watched me interestedly as I said, "Did I or did I not hear you say that Grubb had actually been spotted in the area of the murder scene a day or two *before* the killing, and he *might* have been there on the day Eric was killed?"

"That's what I said."

"I don't know about that, Captain."

"I'd rather have him on the trail on the day of the crime, yes. But we don't know that he wasn't there on the day of the murder, either. Grubb is certainly unable or unwilling to show that he was anywhere else at the time."

"Anyway," I said, "wasn't Eric bludgeoned to death? Grubb apparently likes to stick knives in people. What about the Saranac Lake assaults? Did he use a knife or a club?"

"He threatened people with knives, and hit one with a rock."

"Oh."

"Eric Osborne was hit from behind, on the head, thirty or thirty-one times, with a heavy blunt instrument that left no residue. That rules out a log or branch or other barky natural object of the forest. The handle end of a golf club is a possibility. The object was roughly of that thickness. It appears that the perpetrator was hiding behind some rock ledge, jumped out just as Eric passed by, and pounded away. Eric probably never knew what hit him."

"Whoever did it," I said, "obviously wanted to make sure that Eric was dead."

"That's so. It was a vicious attack by someone in a great fury."

"And by someone who, it sounds like, carried the murder weapon with him or her on the trail. How far off the road did the crime occur?"

"Less than a mile," Stankie said. "The weapon was never found, but Grubb could have stashed it in his camping gear and trekked out to 418 and thumbed a ride. That's generally how he got around. So far, we've been unable to locate the motorist who gave him a lift out of the area."

"Was Osborne robbed?" I asked.

"Apparently not. At any rate, nothing obvious was lifted from his wallet. But then we don't know what all Eric had in his possession at the time."

"Then that's another reason to discount Grubb, who seems to like to hurt and rob strangers. Captain, you've got sixteen people who were on that trail around the time of the killing. But how do you know there weren't others? Especially since the murder took place so close to Route 418."

He shrugged. "We don't."

"Who knew Eric was going hiking that day, and where he planned on walking? Anybody?"

Stankie fidgeted with his folder and said, "As a matter of fact, quite a few people knew."

"Uh-huh."

"Every Monday morning, Eric hiked up to Hobbs Pond, where he'd spend several hours watching a beaver clan he'd been writing about in his Thursday column in the *Herald*. It was a series he'd started in late March. Twenty-two thousand copies of the *Herald* are sold every day, so—you can take it from there, Mr. Strachey. That opens up other possibilities—I realize that. But possibilities are possibilities, and evidence is evidence, and the best evidence still points to Gordon Grubb— a known violent killer, probably a psychopath—as Osborne's assailant. Of course, the case is officially open. And so's my mind."

Stankie sat watching me with a look that seemed to suggest he was waiting for me to say something, but I had no idea what it was he wanted me to say. When I asked, "What have you heard from the sheriff's department on the two Jet Ski attacks?" Stankie looked almost disappointed.

He said, "The Jet Skier got away yesterday, but Sheriff Stone has a sketchy description of a pickup truck that somebody saw near the north end of the lake not long after the attack. This guy had a Jet Ski in the back of his truck and was speeding east. They haven't got a plate number, only a general description of the truck, so I don't know whether anything much is going to come of that. The sheriff tells me he's going to be keeping an eye on Janet's place for a while, but he's advised her to stay off the lake for the time being and she's agreed to play it safe."

"She and Dale Kotlowicz are staying in town at the Osborne family house for now, and I'm there with them."

"Good," Stankie said, and again he looked as if he were waiting for me to ask some critical question I'd neglected to ask so far, or to open up a topic he felt unable to introduce on his own.

I said, "The Osbornes are quite a family. I'd never met any of them before."

"They are, aren't they?" Now he was alert.

"Three generations of American overachievers."

"I'd put it at about two-and-a-half," Stankie said. "And the fourth generation you can pretty much forget about."

"I haven't met any of the fourth generation yet."

"And chances are, you won't."

"Why's that?"

He eyed me grimly. "Dick and June Puderbaugh have two boys, Titus—he's called Tidy—and Frederick, who's better known as Tacker. Tacker left town four years ago, no loss to Edensburg. He was an aimless, slow-witted boy who always seemed to be in the vicinity of trouble—one of his best buddies is doing time at Ossining for dealing coke in a school zone. The last I heard of Tacker, he was a beach bum in Fiji or someplace out in the South Seas.

"Tidy, the older boy, is here in town, and theoretically he practices law, but if he's ever had a client, I couldn't tell you who it would be. Tidy and three other nicely manicured, underemployed youths with fat trust funds spend seven afternoons a week in an alcove off the grill-room at the Edensburg Country Club, where they have their own table for an ongoing bridge game. The only way you'll get to meet Tidy is by crashing his game or by ambushing him when he's on his way in or out of his condo at Pleasant Meadow Estates.

"Tidy lives out there in an apartment that adjoins the condo of Ann Marie Consolati, who runs a body-waxing and electrolysis hair-removal parlor in town. I've been reliably informed by a friend in the construction business that there's a hidden door that opens between Tidy's clothes closet and Ann Marie's—even though Tidy has been engaged to Debbie Stockton, the boat-cushion heiress, for six years. And I can also tell you—although I cannot divulge my source of information on this point—that Tidy Puderbaugh does not have a single hair on his body from the neck down."

Stankie colored a little as he mentioned this eccentrically lubricious detail and cracked a droll little smile. Then, looking instantly somber again, he said, "Tacker's a sad loser, and Tidy is ineffectual and a little bit comical, but Chester and Pauline Osborne's son, Craig, should not be taken lightly at all. Craig Osborne is highly intelligent, shrewd as they come, and altogether ruthless. He's in Attica doing twenty-five to life for killing a guard in a diamond heist last year. Before that, Craig had a record as long as your arm for robberies and assaults and god-knows-what-all, going back to when he was just twelve years old. Craig Osborne, I can tell you, is a thirty-year-old man with no moral conscience whatsoever, and I'd say he is capable of just about anything."

Stankie stopped talking and looked at me again—as if I were somehow supposed to supply the point of his discourse on Tacker, Tidy, and Craig. I said, "Craig couldn't possibly have been Eric's killer, could he?"

Stankie shook his head and kept watching me. "Nunh-unh," he said.

"When was Craig sent up?"

"December tenth, and he'd been in custody since June of last year, when he was wounded in a shoot-out at the jewel heist in Tarrytown." He looked at me some more.

"Why are you telling me this?" I finally said.

Stankie leaned forward and said quietly, "Eric Osborne was a fine young man."

"That's what I keep hearing."

"If Grubb didn't kill him, I want the man who did kill him apprehended."

"Good."

He said, "A snitch at Attica reported that Craig Osborne talked about Eric's death and said there was more to it than the investigators knew." Stankie was motionless, but now he seemed to be watching two things: me and the door behind me, which opened into an outer office and was ajar.

Stankie said, "This got back to me through channels, and I asked that the snitch press for details. He claimed to the warden out there that he wasn't able to pry anything else out of Osborne."

"That's too bad," I said. "Maybe it was just talk, a sociopath's braggadocio."

"That could be. But Craig said one other thing to the snitch that might give you pause. It did me. On one occasion, Craig was talking about Eric's murder and how there was more to it than the investigation had turned up, and he made a crack to the snitch about his own murder conviction and how, 'Anyway, offing people runs in the Osborne family.' Those were the words he used: 'Offing people runs in the Osborne family.'"

"I've heard about a tendency toward violence in some Watsons and Osbornes. But the jewel guard's was the only actual homicide by an Osborne, according to Janet."

"It's the only one I know of," Stankie said. "Of course, Chester, Craig's father, has a couple of assaults in his record—or did, before they were erased."

"I heard about that too. And I've met Chester. He's creepy enough."

"There's an Osborne intrafamily fight going on," Stankie said in a matter-of-fact way. "It's over the ownership of the *Herald*. Eight million dollars is at stake, plus, of course, the paper's reputation. You're up-to-date on that, I take it."

"I am."

"And the ins and outs of the upcoming board of directors' vote, and how Eric's death means one less vote for selling the *Herald* to a quality newspaper chain at a loss to the family of eight million dollars."

"Funny you should mention that, Captain. It's exactly the angle on this whole thing—Eric's murder and the two Jet Ski attacks—that a number of people close to the situation are currently considering." I said, "Are Craig and his father close?"

"They seem not to be," Stankie said. "In fact, Chester disowned Craig a long time ago. But I can tell you confidentially, Mr. Strachey, that Chester Osborne has visited Craig in Attica twice in the past five months, once just before Eric's death in mid-May, and again on June fourteenth."

"I see. Is there anything else you'd like to tell me confidentially, Captain?"

"No. Just that I can't carry the Osborne-family angle of the investigation any further than I have. I can't question Craig without betraying the Attica snitch, who is considered too valuable an asset for the warden out there to transfer. I can't question Chester because I have no evidence whatsoever connecting anybody but Gordon Grubb to Eric's murder, and Chester is liable to accuse me of spreading false rumors about himself and the Puderbaughs. He'll have some State Street lawyer down in Albany visiting the commissioner and threatening to sue me for slander." Again, he waited.

"So what do you expect me to do?" I said. "The investigative work of the New York State Police?"

"Yeah, I'm kind of hoping you will," he said. "Of course, I can't be of any assistance to you, or be associated with your work in any way. Until, of course, you nail that arrogant asshole Chester Osborne. Then I'll see he's strung up real good."

"Oh, so you know Chester pretty well then?"

"We went to school together," Stankie said. "We played on the same varsity hockey team for three seasons, in fact—until the day at practice when I checked Chester for the third time that afternoon and he turned around and pounded me in the face with his stick so hard that he knocked all my teeth out."

Stankie opened his mouth and popped out a double set of dentures, uppers and lowers.

12

Stu Torkildson and Chester Osborne kept me waiting in Torkildson's outer office ten minutes past our 9:30 appointment time, giving me a chance to peruse that day's *Herald*. I looked over the thoughtful mix for which the *Herald* was esteemed—national and international news from *The New York Times* and *Washington Post–L.A. Times* news services, clearly written and carefully edited local stories on matters that affected people's lives, editorial and op-ed pages with commentaries that were both serious and lively. Parson Bates's column, "Our Eden," ran that day too. In it, Bates attacked the "multiculturalist" Tex-Mex items cropping up in recent months on the menus of so many local restaurants. He wrote that he couldn't understand why people wanted to eat food that made their necks sweat. Public neck sweating was put forth as yet another symptom of the nation's moral rot.

Chester Osborne was there in his stockbroker's outfit when I was ushered into Stu Torkildson's office. Osborne gazed at me morosely and didn't get up from his chair, but Torkildson came over and twinkled with approval at the sight of me.

"It's the investigatory man of the year," he said, and squeezed my hand and grinned as if I were a long-lost Dartmouth fraternity brother.

"That's a view not unanimously held in Edensburg," I said, tossing Chester a quick look. "But thanks for the vote of confidence, Mr. Torkildson."

"I'm Stu," he said.

"I'm Don."

And that was Chester over there sulking.

"Coffee?" Torkildson said.

"Black," I said.

He didn't buzz for his secretary, as many men of his station might have, but personally maneuvered a carafe and a mug with the *Herald*'s logo on it. Torkildson was sixty or so, starting to settle around the middle, but still solid looking in a well-cut dark suit, blue shirt, and polka-dot bow tie. His black loafers gleamed, as did his pate, which was as bald as a rapper's and as carefully waxed and tended. He was a phrenologist's dream—not that I was tempted to ask him to bend down so that I could study his bumps. He had a wide, pleasant face that was as hairless as his head, and a warm, steady gaze that could have meant he was without guile, or it could have been the practiced affectation of the craftiest man in Edensburg. I wondered, but not for long, which it might be.

"I was sorry to hear about your friend Timothy hurting himself yesterday," Torkildson said. He took the one empty chair by the coffee table—Chester occupied the other one—and I got the low couch. "I was happy to hear that the injury wasn't serious, but the incident must have been frightening for both of you."

"It was. It looked as if the Jet Skier was trying hard to run somebody down—almost certainly Janet, since the same thing happened last week when she was on the lake herself."

"Janet always did have an overly active imagination," Chester said sourly.

Torkildson gave me a genial don't-mind-him look and said, "Chester is the skeptic in the Osborne family."

A tendency he'd been known to express with a hockey stick. I said, "The police are taking the incident seriously, as they ought to. It was either gross negligence or attempted murder—serious stuff, either way."

"I couldn't agree more," Torkildson said, and Osborne sniffed and shook his head. "I saw Janet when she came in this morning," Torkildson went on, "and while she's one tough cookie, she's been badly shaken by yesterday's events. I've known Janet for more than thirty years, and I think I know when that girl is hurting. I talked to her, and I hope I was able to pep her up some."

"Did Janet discuss her suspicions with you?" I said. "That Eric's murder and the Jet Ski attacks might be related to each other and to the fight over control of the *Herald*?"

Osborne slumped low in his seat looking glum, but Torkildson said

88

conversationally, "No, Janet and I spoke only briefly, but Chester has filled me in on that aspect of the story. It's pretty lurid stuff for Edensburg, I have to tell you." He grinned and made mock shivering noises. "Sounds more like a thriller you'd pick up at the airport than real life, to be perfectly candid."

I said, "No, it sounds to me more like real life—a valuable family asset being fought over by too many heirs, all of whom have different values, and varying motives for either holding on to an asset or disposing of it in one way or another, and some of whom are desperate in their need for one outcome or another. And once in a while, in situations like this one, that desperation turns murderous. It happens. History is full of it, and newspapers are too. Even the *Herald,* I'll bet, sometimes reports on family members obliterating other family members over money."

Osborne glared at me and said, "This is actionable. Strachey, if you talk garbage like that outside this room, I'll see *you* in *court!*"

Torkildson must have been used to Chester's eruptions and appeared unfazed. He said, "Chettie, I can see why you're ticked off—I'm sure I would be too if I were in your shoes. But try to understand that Don here is an outsider coming into a situation where he's unfamiliar with the lay of the land, and he's feeling his way. The first people he talks to are people who've suffered a tragic loss, and on top of that they've had the daylights scared out of them by some nitwit on the lake who ought to be barred for life from going anywhere near a device with an internal combustion engine attached to it. Naturally this one-sided combination is going to suggest that the *Herald'*s current situation will represent a legitimate line of inquiry into these other difficult matters.

"So, on the one hand, Don's pursuing that line of inquiry is entirely understandable. While on the other hand, however, there's the indisputable fact that no evidence exists tying these violent acts to the Osborne family's disagreements over the *Herald'*s disposition. There's been a lot of emotion, and that's led to certain fears, but a professional investigator like Don here, Chettie, is not about to be swayed by fear and emotion." Torkildson looked me in the eye and smiled and said, "For a pro like yourself, it always has to be, 'Just the facts, if you please, ma'am.' Have I got it right, Don?"

It was like listening to the Okefenokee Swamp talk. I was surprised Torkildson had never run successfully for national office. Nor could I respond to Torkildson's verbal miasma with crisp candor. Bringing up Chester's ominous and suggestive threat to his mother—in order to prevent the *Herald*'s sale to the good chain, "somebody else might have to get hurt"—would only have provoked a furious denial from Chester. And Captain Bill Stankie's report on Chester's two prison visits to the son he had supposedly disowned—and who had hinted to another Attica inmate that an Osborne family member had been involved in Eric's murder—was confidential. My repeating the report would both betray Stankie's trust and trigger who knew what kind of unwanted-at-this-point hysterical reaction on the part of Chester Osborne.

So I said to Torkildson: "Stu, you make an excellent case for open-mindedness, and open-minded is what I plan to be. But tell me, besides the conflict over the *Herald,* can you think of any other reason why anyone would try to kill Janet? There is evidence that the Jet Ski attacks were not accidental. The skier came at her on two separate occasions. He made repeated runs at her the first time—last week—and two runs yesterday, which I witnessed myself. Why might anybody do that, do you think?"

Osborne shifted in his seat and muttered, "Jealous dykes, if you ask me."

"I'm wondering what Stu thinks," I said. "He knows Janet well—works with her every day."

Torkildson screwed up his face. "Of course, I don't keep an eye on Janet's private life at all, you have to understand. And at the *Herald* the business and editorial sides of the paper are separate, so days will go by when we don't even see one another. But my impression is that Janet and Dale are a devoted couple. So it seems unlikely that these attacks—and I'll take your word that that's what you think they were—were the work of some type of crazed lesbian. Otherwise—what? A disgruntled former employee? I suppose the *Herald* has a few of those out there . . . every business does. Janet herself would be the one to ask about that, I would guess. Or Bob Comongore, our director of human resources. Perhaps it was an outraged reader." Torkildson chuckled and said, "I know we've got one or two of those. Although generally a testy letter to the editor lances any boil growing on the average incensed reader's butt. Attempted murder by an irate reader would be a first, in my experience."

I said, "What about Eric's murder?"

"It broke our hearts," Torkildson said without hesitation. "Eric Osborne was one of the finest human beings it has ever been my honor to know."

"Why is he bringing that up?" Chester whined. "Do you see what I mean, Stu? Let's put this all in the hands of a good attorney before this guy runs roughshod."

"Don, why *are* you bringing Eric into this?" Torkildson said coolly. "In his case, there couldn't have been any connection to the *Herald* situation. Eric was murdered, according to the State Police, by a serial killer who went on to attack other outdoors people in Pennsylvania. Are you suggesting there's even the possibility that this Gordon Grubb character was an agent of one of the parties in the disagreement over the *Herald*'s disposition?"

"No," I said, "that sounds farfetched. But the evidence against Grubb is sketchy and circumstantial. He was actually last spotted near the murder scene a full two days before Eric was killed. The police say that Grubb admits to nothing, and the case is still open. I met with the investigating officer, Bill Stankie, earlier this morning, and while he considers Grubb his prime suspect, that's *all* Grubb is. Stankie is open to following any actual evidence that turns up, wherever it might lead."

I watched Chester Osborne when I mentioned Stankie's name; his face tightened and his mouth formed a hard little button.

"Don, now that's exactly my point," Torkildson said. "Legally the case against Grubb is circumstantial, yes—as are most murder cases that result in convictions. But the police suspect Grubb because there is no evidence whatsoever, circumstantial or otherwise, linking anyone else to the crime. I wouldn't go so far as to term any linkage between Eric's death and the *Herald*'s situation a paranoid fantasy—or, as Chester seems to regard it, a malicious and actionable accusation. But the idea does necessitate a quite severe stretch of the imagination, considering that not a shred of evidence exists to support such an egregious criminal linkage.

"In journalism, as you may have heard, Don, we take immense care to check our facts before we send them out into the world. At the *Herald,* we have a three-independent-sources rule on matters as important as—conspiracy to commit murder is what we're talking about here, and that's a capital crime in the state of New York. Now, you're going here and there spreading this idea of members of the Osborne family involved in a conspiracy to murder without—correct me if I'm wrong—even a single source to support your speculation? That's thin, mighty thin, and it would not pass muster even at newspapers with ethical standards one heck of a lot lower than the *Herald*'s. This I can tell you without fear of contradiction by the Pulitzer board. It's an awfully slender limb you've climbed out onto, ethically speaking, and I think the question you've got to be asking yourself, Don, is this: 'What dire result might accrue, to the Osbornes, to the *Herald,* or to myself?'

"You know, Don, an awful lot is at stake in the outcome of the disposition of the *Herald*. On that point, you're right on the money. And as you may know, I favor the paper's sale to Crewes-InfoCom. Harry Griscomb's is a fine organization, but with newspaper publishing costs escalating the way they are, Griscomb won't survive for long in this climate. So why shouldn't the Osbornes come out of this unhappy situation with a few dollars to the family name? I'd say, after more than a hundred years' dedicated effort and high-minded community stewardship, they've earned it. Both InfoCom and Griscomb, I should also point out, are sensitive about their public images—Griscomb maybe even more so than InfoCom—and either buyer could become suddenly skittish if word got back to them that a business deal they were attempting to complete involved—or suddenly was reported to have involved—a conspiracy to commit murder. Neither bid is binding, and I personally wouldn't want to wake up one day to discover that all bids had been withdrawn and that Griscomb and InfoCom had stopped taking my calls. The tragic upshot of that would be the *Herald* company's creditors would seize the paper in September and sell it to the highest bidder—probably InfoCom—and the paper would be gone and the family would end up with zip.

"Now, do you want that to happen, Don? Does Janet? Talk to her, is my best advice. Explain the situation, and see if Janet doesn't agree that the best course for both the *Herald* and all the Osbornes at this point is for you to drop your well-intentioned but potentially explosively disruptive investigation, and for you to pack your bags and head on back down to Albany. If Janet is afraid for her safety or her mother's or Dan's, a good private security firm can be brought on board to allay their fears until the *Herald* directors meet on September eighth. But as for this Oliver Stone-style conspiracy-to-murder scenario that's boiling away and threatening to blow up in everybody's face, I'd put a lid on that real fast if I were you. This may not be what you want to hear from me, Don. I realize that. But it's my best advice, and I'd be an s.o.b. if I didn't give it to you straight. That's what I do. It's what I'm paid for. It's how I've made my way in Edensburg, and I think Janet will tell you, what I have to say is as worth listening to today as it was back when Tom Osborne was winning Pulitzers and the *Herald* was the envy of American journalism. Do you hear what I'm saying, Don? Do you catch my drift? Do you comprehend the extraordinarily high risks here for so many good people, and for yourself?"

The swamp thing ceased burbling and sat watching me with an unctuous grin. Chester sat there looking sly, as if finally I had been boxed up and sealed for delivery out of Edensburg. I thought, Why had Torkildson rattled on and on about a conspiracy to commit murder? I hadn't mentioned anything about a plot involving more than one person. I'd thought it, but I hadn't mentioned it.

I did not speak my thoughts aloud. Instead, I said to Torkildson, "If your advice is so wise and farseeing, Stu, how come your advice in 1988 resulted in the *Herald* sliding into the ugly fix it's in now? You're the last man in the world I'd come to for advice about the *Herald,* or about anything else—except, maybe, where to shop for a bow tie. But thanks, anyway."

Chester sat twitching with rage. But Torkildson gazed at me thoughtfully as I bade them so long until we met again, which I knew beyond a reasonable doubt that we would.

13

Before I left the Herald Building, I stopped in Janet's office and gave her a rundown on my meeting with Chester and Stu Torkildson. She asked if Torkildson had either sold me a souvenir dinner plate from Spruce Haven or picked my pocket. I held out both hands and said, "No plate." My wallet was still in my pocket too.

"Did Chester say anything else about having Mom locked up?" Janet asked.

"It didn't come up. Chester was in with Torkildson when I arrived, so Torkildson might have told him to shut up about that. Or, Chester's threats last night could have been empty bluster. Or, Chester's threats could have been part of a calculated attempt to spook you and your mother into some precipitous action that could be used against you legally, and Torkildson knew all about it but didn't want to be associated with it and if I'd brought it up he'd have acted surprised. But they didn't bring it up, and I wanted to avoid discussion of it until I heard what your lawyer advised."

"I spoke with Slim Finn fifteen minutes ago," Janet said, looking anxious, "and he said that as long as Mom isn't a danger to herself or others, nobody can haul her off against her will or mine. However, they might conceivably get a judge to entertain the idea that she's incapable of carrying out her legal duties as a director of the Herald Corporation. A judge might issue an order blocking Mom's vote, or even forcing her removal from the board. The result, of course, could be Tidy coming onto the board and voting for InfoCom, and the paper would be sunk."

"Couldn't Finn stall a court order until after September eighth? Surely there's some legal cloud of ink he could spew out, leaving the other side thrashing around uselessly for a month or so. There are even those who claim that this is what lawyers are for."

"Maybe it could be done or maybe not," Janet said. "There's so much at stake in this board vote, Slim says, that a judge might be obliged to act immediately. Otherwise, the vote on the sale of the paper would have to be postponed, and if that happened, the bank holding the mortgage might refuse to wait and simply seize the *Herald*. And nobody involved wants that."

I said, "Who's in line for the board seat if a vacancy opens up—your mother's seat or yours or Dan's—and Tidy for some reason can't serve? I'm not offering to knock off Tidy or have him kidnapped to Bishkek. I'm just interested to know what the line of succession is, in case there's another pro-Griscomb vote somewhere down the line that you might now be maneuvering into position as plan B."

Janet shook her head. "Chester's son, Craig, is next in line after Tidy, but he's in prison and the company by-laws stipulate that board members must be present in order to vote. Which is too bad, because Craig hates Chester so much he'd probably vote for Griscomb just to get back at his father."

"Get back at him for what?"

Janet hesitated. She looked almost flustered, which was out of character for her. She said, "You've met Chester." She gazed at me sorrowfully.

"I have. He's not ideal parent material."

She said, "It's worse than that."

"Oh."

"I think he beat Craig."

"You think so?"

"Eric and Dan and I always suspected it. But we never felt we had enough evidence to confront Chester or to bring in an outsider to investigate. The injuries were never that serious—no broken bones or internal injuries that we knew of. But that kid had more bruises than any child I ever saw, and he acted like an abused kid: uncommunicative, withdrawn, listless.

"And then, of course, there's the circumstantial evidence of the way Craig turned out. From adolescence on, he was a liar, a thief, and a fighter—a dirty fighter too, according to word around town. In hindsight, somebody in the family should have stepped in, and maybe we could have saved Craig from wrecking his life. Twenty-five years ago, of course, child abuse wasn't as recognizable as it is today, or taken as seriously by the law or society. Back then, a parent could get away with treating his child in a way that, if he treated anybody else's kid that way, he'd be convicted of assault and sent to prison for years. Still, some of us did suspect what was going on, and now I wish we'd tried to intervene."

I said, "Physical abusers were usually abused themselves when they were young. Was that true of Chester?"

Janet blushed and said, "Uhn-uhn. No."

"You're sure?"

She shuddered. "I'm sure. Your suggesting it is disconcerting, though. Neither Mom nor Dad was particularly affectionate toward— or effusive in their expressions of approval of—any of us. And Dad was particularly hard on—even cold with—Chester. Chettie was the oldest, and when it turned out he had no interest in the journalism profession—acquisitiveness was Chester's main interest in life from about the age of three—Dad had no more use for Chester. I think I can safely say he didn't like him. And it showed. Dad's characteristic way with Chester was either to ignore him—that's the way it was most of the time—or to snap at Chettie over niggling matters.

"Was there physical abuse? No. Can you term what I just described as psychological abuse? Maybe. Although, if it is, the legislatures had better not make it a felony without first spending billions of dollars on more prison cells. From what I've observed, as a style of parenting it comes dangerously close to being the norm in this country. Not that the current Congress is about to outlaw it, of course. Among the traditional family values cherished by the religious right, emotional abuse is surely high up in their pantheon, if their own biographies are any guide."

I said, "Your overall assessment of family life in America, Janet, seems to me unduly bleak. Anyway, you and Eric both turned out emotionally healthy. That must have come from somewhere in the Osborne family."

A wistful smile. "I guess so. They say every child experiences the same family differently. Eric's and my peculiarities—and our interests—were much more in tune with Mom's and Dad's than Chester's were, or June's. Even our both turning out gay seemed to fit in with the Osborne tradition of defiant rugged individualism. On the other hand, June, the social-climbing ditz, was never appreciated for who she was. And of course as Chester's tendencies toward violence surfaced, that didn't particularly endear him or add to his opportunities in the family dynamic."

"And you think it's possible that what Chester experienced as psychological abuse in your parents' home was so traumatic that he passed it on in his own home as physical abuse?"

She said, "I'm afraid so."

I asked Janet if I'd heard correctly the day before when I thought she said that Chester had "disowned" Craig—meaning presumably that their disaffection was so complete that they no longer had any contact with each other at all.

"That's the impression I have," she said. "It's certainly the impression Chester leaves on those rare occasions when anybody dares mention Craig's name in Chester's presence."

I said, "Then why would Chester have visited Craig at Attica twice in the last twelve weeks?"

She stared hard. "He did? Chester visited Craig in prison?"

I nodded. "It's important to my source, a good guy who wants to keep his job, that you don't repeat this."

"All right." I could all but hear the wheels whirring inside her head.

To protect the Attica warden's informant, I did not repeat the—possibly unreliable—hearsay evidence of Craig telling the prison snitch that there was more to Eric Osborne's death than the investigators knew and that at least one homicide had been commited by a member of the family other than Craig. But I did say: "With his criminal history and criminal connections—and now with these unexplained visits from his suddenly not-so-alienated father—Craig at least bears looking into. I may drive out there and interview him myself."

She still looked dumbfounded. "Well . . . I just don't know what to think."

"If somehow Tidy is unable to serve on the *Herald* board of directors," I said, "and Craig can't do it on account of being locked up, who's next in line to move on to the board? Anybody helpful to the good-chain cause?"

"It would be Tidy's brother, Tacker Puderbaugh. But he's no factor, believe me, Don. Tacker has no interest whatever in the *Herald*. He's already got enough money from his trust fund from Grandmother Watson's estate to meet his minimal needs—a bathing suit and a supply of surfboard wax, as I understand it. And anyway, Tacker was ten thousand miles from Edensburg, the last I knew. He spent one semester at the University of Hawaii in 1990, then started drifting southwestward, and he just kept on drifting."

"Do you have his current address?"

"I can get it from—Tidy would be the best bet. If I asked June, she'd be suspicious."

"I think we need to confirm that Tacker is in fact halfway around the world and uninvolved in the struggle here. Any financial interest he might have in the *Herald*'s disposition would be indirect—through June—but real enough. After Tidy and Tacker, who's next in line for a board seat?"

"That's it as far as the family is concerned. None of us were big followers of the Holy Scriptures, and the Osbornes don't seem to have gone forth and multiplied at a rate anywhere near the world average. The company by-laws state that if no direct descendant of Daniel Lincoln Osborne is able or willing to serve on the *Herald*'s board, the existing board can fill a vacancy with a nonfamily member of the board's choosing. The board as it's now constituted, of course, would pick somebody who's pro-Griscomb. But that's all academic, isn't it? Tidy is in good health, as far as I know, and it's unlikely he'll meet a violent end in the grillroom at the country club. Even if Tidy got one, a puncture wound from the toothpick in a BLT is rarely fatal."

When I'd entered her office twenty minutes earlier, Janet had shut off the ringer on her office phone and activated her voice mail. The voice-mail light had been blinking for several minutes, and now a tiny woman with a pixie cut whom I recognized from the newsroom stuck her head in Janet's open door and said, "Sorry to interrupt, but Dale wants you to call her at your mother's house. She said to tell you that your Mom is okay, but there is some kind of urgent situation."

"What kind? Is June out there with a lawyer?"

"No, she didn't mention that. It has something to do with Dan. He had a close call this morning, Dale said."

"Oh, hell, that nails it," Janet said. She snatched up the phone with one hand and her handbag with the other.

14

It was *exactly* like Karen Silkwood," Arlene Thurber said, as she accepted the joint Dan passed to her and took a deep toke. Then she offered the reefer around the Osborne back porch where six of us were seated. One by one, Timmy, Dale, Janet, and I shook our heads no thanks. Elsie the housekeeper was upstairs helping Ruth Osborne clean out a closet; just as well.

"It was *sooo* weird," Arlene went on in a voice that was faster than slo-mo but not quite normal speed, either. "I mean, it was just yesterday I was saying that all this crazy shit that's going down—I mean Eric getting killed and that Jet Ski attack—that all that shit sounds *exactly* like Karen Silkwood. I said that yesterday, and then—holy smokes!— what happens? Somebody tries to run Dan and me off the road and take us out, just like Kerr-McGhee did to Karen Silkwood! Can you believe this crazy shit?"

Dale said, "We can believe it."

Arlene had just described how she and Dan had been driving early that morning on a rural county road. At a spot where the road ran along a woodsy hillside, a large pickup truck had sped up behind them and repeatedly banged into the rear of Dan's Range Rover. It was obvious, Arlene said, that the truck was trying to force their car off the right shoulder down a steep embankment. Constantly in danger of losing control, Dan was able to keep the vehicle on the road for a half mile before he veered too far into the oncoming traffic lane, did lose control, and ran off the left side of the road and along a ditch.

The car ended up nose down in the basin next to a drainage culvert. Dan and Arlene had been wearing seat belts and were unhurt, but the Range Rover was badly damaged, probably totaled, Dan thought. The pickup truck had then sped on up the rural road. Ten minutes later, a man on his way home from an early-morning trout-fishing excursion came along and drove Dan and Arlene to a main-road gas station, where they phoned the State Police. Two officers soon arrived and took them back to the crash site, questioned them there, and then brought them back into town. A tow truck had been dispatched for the wrecked Range Rover.

I said, "Did you mention to the cops our ideas about a possible connection between Eric's murder and the Jet Ski attacks and now this?"

"*I* certainly did," Arlene said, her voice full of mellow outrage. Dan sat slumped in a wicker chair, his head back and his eyes squeezed shut. "Dan thought maybe we should cool it," Arlene went on, "on account of where we'd just been when the attack happened. But I thought no, we don't have to mention that, but we can still be up front about this other bad shit. I mean, how else can the cops help us if we don't share our thoughts and feelings with them?" Arlene nudged Dan, who opened his eyes and accepted the smoldering joint from her. Timmy had on a mild huff-huff look, but he kept his lip buttoned. Dale must have noticed this, for at one point she did accept one toke, exhaling grandiosely in Timmy's direction.

Janet said, "So, where had you two been when the attack happened? Not burglarizing hunting cabins, I hope."

"Don't be absurd," Dan said disgustedly.

"I'm only asking because Arlene said you couldn't tell it to the police. Any suggestion that you were involved in something illegal this morning is not ridiculous at all, Dan."

"We'd just been out to see our dealer," Arlene said good-naturedly, waggling her eyebrows and indicating the reefer. "We had two ounces of sensi buds stashed under the backseat. The way the cops would have acted if they'd found it—you'd think we were criminals or something. Anyway, we left the whole stash in a tree near where we crashed. We'll have to go out there later and pick up the sensi before some animal gets at it."

I said, "Were you able to get a look at the truck and driver? I realize your focus was on the road in front of you and trying to stay on it."

102

"That's right, it was," Dan said sarcastically. "Taking notes somehow slipped our minds."

"The truck was red," Arlene said. "That much I can remember. Dan had his eyes glued to the road, naturally, but I looked back a couple times, and the truck had a black grill with horizontal bars. I couldn't see the driver because the truck was right on top of us, and our back window is low, and he was too high up. And then when we ran off the road we were bouncing all over the place, and by the time we got stopped, the truck had gone around a bend. But I do remember that it was big and it was red."

"Like the pickup somebody saw speeding away from the lake yesterday with the Jet Ski in the back," Janet said, and we all nodded gravely and considered this data.

Dale asked, "Who knew you'd be out on that road early this morning, Arlene?"

"Just Liver," Arlene said.

When she seemed to have nothing to add to that, Timmy said, "Your marijuana dealer's name is Liver?"

"Liver Livingston. His real name is Samuel. He told us his family used to have a railroad or a canal or something, but now he says they all sell dope."

Dale said, "Was he nicknamed Liver because he loves life, or after the organ?"

Arlene made a "beats me" face, but Dan said, "I once heard his nickname came from his favorite food. In any case, I doubt that Liver would appreciate our sitting around discussing him in connection with somebody trying to kill Arlene and me. In fairness to Liver, let's just try to leave him out of this." Arlene relit the joint while Dan held it with a roach clip he'd pulled out of the pocket of his work shirt.

I said, "Are you telling us, Dan, that if somebody asked Liver for a schedule of when you might be traveling the isolated road out to his place, he'd have refused to provide it?"

"That's exactly what I'm telling you. Yes."

"You have every reason to trust him, and no reason not to?"

"Liver Livingston and I," Dan said solemnly, "have been friends for more than twenty years. Not just friends—brothers. We've worked in the cane fields of Cuba together. We went to the mountains of

Nicaragua together. We are *compañeros*. Does that answer your question?"

I said, "I can understand why you trust Liver. But the man is in what I think you'll concede is an iffy line of work. Rightly or wrongly, Liver's trade is a criminal enterprise in the state of New York. People who do what he does make enemies. Even if you accept the idea that there's no chance he would ever have set you up, isn't it possible that another dealer might be attempting to muscle in on Liver's territory by scaring away his customers?"

Arlene blurted out, "What an asshole that would be!"

Dan seemed to roll this idea around in his head for some seconds, as if he was interested in the sound of it but couldn't quite bring himself to endorse the theory. Finally, he said, "No, I would seriously doubt that. Liver is a small-time guy whose gross is peanuts. He takes in enough to get by—it's just Liver and Patsy and their old dog out there—and he sees himself predominantly as a good citizen providing a public service. Who could possibly want to use violence to take over an operation like that?"

I caught Timmy's eye—I guessed we were both wondering what Liver's dog's name might be—and then I looked at Dan and said, "Given what's happened to you and Janet lately—and to Eric in May—I share your opinion that the incident today had nothing to do with Liver. What it looks an awful lot like is another episode in a plot to alter the *Herald* board of directors' vote on September eighth. But to be sure, I wish you'd get in touch with Liver, Dan, and describe your close call today and ask him if anything like it has happened to any of his other customers. Ask him too whether he's heard anything like what happened to you and Arlene happening to other people who travel that road."

Dan sniffed and said, "Oh, sure. I'll call him. Why not? Since you and Janet are running the Osbornes' family affairs now, I guess I'd better just do as I'm told."

Janet slapped the wicker table next to her and barked, "Damn it, Dan, that is *so* unfair—"

But Dale was holding up a traffic-cop hand and saying, "Wait a minute, wait a minute, wait a minute."

Janet shut her mouth and sat back stewing while Dale went on to make the case that we were all in this together, and ultimately our best interests and highest goals were the same: staying alive and saving the *Herald*. Dale argued that she and Timmy once had had "an ugly run-in with grim consequences for American society," and that since they were managing to get along despite the "moral chasm" that separated them, the rest of us could damn well find a way to get along too.

"What did you two guys fight over?" Arlene asked Dale and Timmy. "I'm surprised. You're both such nice people."

Timmy said, "Good question, Arlene."

"I'll fill you in later, Arlene," Dale said. "Right now we need to concentrate on what happened to you and Dan today, and on how we're going to make sure nothing else like it happens to any of us. Don't you agree, Don?"

I said I agreed, and everybody else nodded with varying degrees of enthusiasm.

Dale looked at Dan and Arlene, who were attempting to get one last ignition out of their reefer, and said, "I think you two ought to consider staying here in the house with us until this thing is over and we can be sure all of us are safe from whoever's been trying to knock off Osbornes. There's plenty of room, we can ask the cops to keep an eye on this place, and if anybody shows up and tries anything here on the premises—well, Don's got a gun, Janet told me, that Timmy brought back from Albany last night."

Arlene screamed. Everybody else jumped, and when they'd collected themselves, I said, "It's a precaution. I've had the NRA firearms safety course—and the United States Army's—and there's no need to be concerned."

Dan said, "I've spent some time around people who found themselves in a position where it was necessary for them to carry weapons, and I understand that this is sometimes unfortunately the case. So if you want to arm yourself, Strachey, and turn this house into a fortified position, that's up to you and Janet. But I can't see that anybody is going to be stupid enough to come after a member of the Osborne family right here in Edensburg. Arlene and I will be safe enough in our apartment. And while I can see the point in keeping an eye on Mom, I think you're in danger of overreacting quite badly otherwise. For what little my opinion is worth, of course."

Arlene gawked at him and said, "Speak for yourself, Dan. I'm scared shitless. I think we should all stay here together where we can take care of each other and share our thoughts and concerns. And, hey, it could even be fun. Corn is in, and we could get some ears and make a big batch of corn chowder. Brownies too. Come on, Dan, let's do it. Don't be such a big drag."

Dan looked directly into Arlene's face and said coldly, "I am not staying here overnight. We've all got more important matters on our minds than some goddamn corn roast."

Arlene sneered and snapped, "Asshole!" Then she shrugged and said, "Well, I'm staying."

"That's up to you," Dan said sourly, but he made no move to depart without Arlene.

While I had them all in one place—and to help get our unruly little band focused on the big picture—I summed up my investigation as it had progressed over the previous thirty-six hours. I described my encounter with June and Parson Bates; my conversation with Ruth Osborne in which she revealed Chester's warning that "somebody else might have to get hurt" to keep the *Herald* from being sold to Griscomb; my visit with Chester, during which he threatened me with legal action for spreading slurs against the Osbornes, and he threatened to have Ruth Osborne declared legally incompetent and removed from the *Herald* board of directors; my meeting with Bill Stankie, where he cast new doubt on the supposed guilt of Gordon Grubb in Eric's murder, and at the same time revealed that Chester had twice visited Craig in prison (again I left out Craig's remarks to the snitch concerning Eric's murder); and my meeting with Chester and Stu Torkildson, where Torkildson kept referring to my suspicions of a conspiracy to commit murder when I had not mentioned these suspicions to either Torkildson or Chester Osborne at all.

As I laid out my findings, everyone on the porch listened with great interest, even Dan. He seemed at several points to be breathing heavily and erratically—particularly when I mentioned Chester's visits to Craig in prison. And as I concluded my remarks, Dan got up quickly and made for the first-floor bathroom just down the hall from the porch.

I was about to ask Arlene why Dan vomited every time the subject of an Osborne violent conspiracy came up, but just then the front doorbell rang and seconds later June was inside the house with a deputy sheriff.

15

How did we ever get mixed up in this?" Timmy said morosely.

I said, "Let me think."

He was laid out on the four-poster in June's old room, and I was at the desk nearby updating my notes. Lunch was to be served in another ten minutes. June had departed an hour earlier, after watching her mother be served with an order to appear for a court proceeding the following Monday, four days away. June and Chester contended that Ruth Osborne was mentally incapable of carrying out her duties as a Herald Corporation board member, and Mrs. Osborne would be expected to demonstrate that she was of sound mind. When she accepted the papers, Mrs. Osborne had looked at her daughter and asked pleasantly, "Are you wearing your retainer, June?"

Timmy said, "My foot is hot and it itches."

"Sorry."

"I don't mean to whine. I realize there are people in this house with bigger problems than a broken foot."

"Go ahead and whine. I would."

"No, you wouldn't. Anyway, we've got enough whiners in this house. What a jerk Dan Osborne is. And Janet is perfectly rational except when she and Dan are in the same room together. Then both of them sound like a couple of twelve-year-olds."

"Dan can bring that out in anybody," I said. "But it's not his pomposity that's the most interest to me. It's his sensitive stomach. Every time the subject of an Osborne family conspiracy to commit murder comes up, Dan heaves."

"I couldn't help noticing that too. But you don't suspect Dan of killing Eric, do you? Why would he?"

"Right. Why would he?"

"I can't think of any reason having to do with the sale of the *Herald*," Timmy said. "Or any other reason, either."

"According to Janet, the Osborne household harbored more than the average amount of emotional deprivation when she and her brothers and sister were growing up. Emotional deprivation led to emotional warfare, and emotional warfare sometimes leads to physical violence. Still, fratricide is extreme and extremely rare, I know. So, no. I don't have any real reason at this point to suspect Dan. But I do plan on gleaning his whereabouts on the afternoon Eric was murdered. And I'd sure like to find out why Dan vomits at the mention of his brother's death. Is it the shock and terrible loss that hits him hard all over again? Is he squeamish? Or does he have some guilty knowledge of the event?"

"Why don't you just ask him?"

"I'm considering doing that, Timothy. I need to get him alone first. I also need to come up with a sufficiently delicate way of phrasing my interrogatory. It won't do to ask, 'Why does mention of your brother's bludgeoning make you puke your guts out, Dan?' "

"That sounds good enough to me, Don. Euphemisms for vomiting are for kindergarten teachers to use, and euphemisms for murder are for heads of state. Just ask him directly, is my advice. Dan's a grown-up."

"He's a grown-up, but he's also a grown-up who acts like he's got some guilty secret that's eating away at his insides. When I confront Dan, I don't want him to clam up even tighter than he is now, and I don't want him to bolt."

"He's highly indignant over being stuck here, he says, but he's not making any move to leave either. I wonder if he *wants* you to find out something important he knows. Maybe he's trying to work up the courage to tell you something, and it's when he gets close to saying it that he throws up."

"Possibly."

"On the other hand, maybe Dan is simply scared to death he's going to be attacked and killed, and that makes him heave. Having somebody try to run your car over a cliff is bound to unsettle your breakfast. I know I'm nervous about all this, and I'm not even on the *Herald*'s board. Here we are, like Chinese Gordon at Khartoum, the Mahdi's turbaned hordes out there just beyond the perimeter tightening the noose, getting ready to come charging in for the coup de grâce. It *is* frightening."

"That's a little overly vivid, Timothy. But I get your point."

"And then there's Dale," he said, throwing his arms back in a gesture of despair. The pom-poms on June's snowy white bedspread trembled.

"Aren't you glad she's on our side?" I said.

"I'll say. I'd hate to have her across the Nile in Omdurman sharpening her panga."

"I like her," I said, "and I think you would too, Timothy, if she hadn't somehow confused you with Jesse Helms or Richard Speck or whoever it is, and treats you accordingly. She's prickly and blunt in ways you'd find refreshing if you weren't the one getting prickled and pummeled. And Dale can obviously spot a phony a mile away."

He writhed. "Yeah, a phony like me."

"Oh, you're obviously much worse than a mere phony. You said yesterday she was starting to seem dimly familiar. Still no luck placing her?"

"Nah. There is something about that head of hair and the face under it—I've seen them both before somewhere, I'm more and more certain. But hard as I try, I cannot remember where."

"Peace Corps? Was she in your India group?"

"No, that I'd remember. Anyway, she's ten years too young."

"You didn't have a falling out in 1969 over competing poultry debeaking techniques in Andhra Pradesh?"

"I have a feeling I've run into Dale more recently than that. I think it had something to do with work—something at the Assembly. It'll come to me soon, I think. Whatever it is, there must be some misunderstanding. I can't imagine that Dale and I would have been on opposite sides of anything very important. I mean, could we have?"

"It seems unlikely. Yet she referred today to a 'moral chasm' between the two of you. And she said you had done something with 'grim consequences for American society.' Whatever it was, it was plainly a big deal to Dale."

Timmy twisted on the bed again, in obvious mental pain. I went over and climbed on June's bed beside him. I placed my mouth close to Timmy's ear and whispered, "Dale has apparently become convinced—and a woman as smart as she is has to have her reasons—that you are actually G. Gordon Liddy, Timothy. It must be your excellent posture, if not something awful you once did, that has led her to confuse the two of you. To her, this is a turn-off. But not to me. I'm excited. Come to me, Gordo. Hold yourself above my flame."

He smiled weakly, but that's as far as his ardor rose. Timmy had been irritated with Dale earlier, and then angry. But now he was haunted. I hadn't been crazy about it when his mind had been full of Skeeter, and now it was time for me to be patient and indulgent while his mind was full of Dale. Luckily, I had plenty to occupy my mind too—a distinguished New York State family whose members apparently were trying to kill one another off for reasons of ideology and/or cash.

16

With fewer than ninety-six hours to go before Monday's court hearing, the pressure was on. Ruth Osborne's mental state was unpredictable; we knew she might show up and argue eloquently on her own behalf that she was as sane as a NASA flight commander, or she might stare vacantly at the judge for half an hour and then remark on the resemblance of a mole on the side of his neck to the star Sigma Octantis.

After a tense lunch where no one but Arlene had much to say—hoisting a sandaled foot onto the edge of the table, she explained to us what each of her Tibetan toe rings signified—I tried to lure Dan aside for a private talk. But he said he and Arlene had to leave immediately to deal with car insurance matters and to rent a "vehicle" until they could buy a new one. They also needed, he said, to drive out to the scene of that morning's car crack-up and retrieve their stash of "buds." Dan did agree to spend the night at the Osborne house, and when I said I'd like to speak with him privately later in the day, he got a queasy look and said sure, maybe, if he had a chance, he'd see.

Both Janet and Bill Stankie had spoken with the Edensburg chief of police, and he agreed to have a patrol car cruise Maple Street periodically during the day and to watch the house from sunset to sunrise. The chief also offered to provide an escort for Dan and Arlene as they went about their errands, but they said no thanks.

After lunch, I went into Tom Osborne's study, cleared a space on the library table, and worked the phone for an hour. Janet had obtained from Tidy an address in Papeete for his brother, Tacker. A Los Angeles investigative agency I'd done business with on a number of occasions had South Pacific contacts, I knew, and the agency agreed, for a fee, to track down Tacker Puderbaugh and establish his whereabouts, currently and on May 15.

I called another contact, a business reporter for *The New York Times* with whom I'd had a brief, hectic affair of between forty-eight and seventy-two hours in the early seventies and been friends with since then. He told me Crewes-InfoCom had a reputation for being stingy and mean, but he'd never heard of them using violent tactics. Its bullying, in acquisitions and as an employer, stayed within the law, as far as the *Times* reporter knew. But he said he'd ask around and get back to me. Harry Griscomb, the owner of the "good chain," had a reputation in media business circles, I was told, for excellent journalism and "unattractive" profit margins. What was "unattractive"? I asked. "Ten percent instead of twenty or thirty," was the reply.

Then I made several calls to the New York State Department of Correctional Services. After forty minutes in and out of telecommunications computer limbo—"Press forty-one to descend from the Purgatoria to the Inferno"—I reached the appropriate office at Attica State Correctional Facility and was able to set up a meeting for the next morning at ten o'clock with Craig Osborne.

Dan and Arlene were off on their car-related errands, and Janet went back to work at the *Herald*. With Timmy and Dale to watch over Ruth Osborne, and a cop car patrolling the neighborhood, I had the rest of the afternoon to roam Edensburg.

The town was, if not an idyllic Rockwellian piece of small-city Americana, still reasonably healthy for the unstable age it had survived into. The (so far) locally owned canoe manufacturing company that had been Edensburg's economic mainstay for over one hundred years had not moved its factory to low-wage, long-hour Ciudad Juárez or Kuala Lumpur; in fact, Janet had told me, the company was doing reasonably well, having diversified into the production of fiberglass bodies for Jet Skis, ORVs, and light-truck bumpers. Tourism brought seasonal work into the area too in summer and during the ski season. Even the *Herald* would have been making a go of it, had it not been for Stu Torkildson's Spruce Haven debacle.

Edensburg's Main Street had only a few vacant storefronts. The four-story department store had been carved up into smaller businesses—

a comic book store, Betty Lou's Hairport, a New Agey place called Crystals n' Constellations, among them—and J. J. Newberry's looked as if it was still going strong despite the competition from the Kmart at the edge of town. A battle to keep Wal-Mart out of the county was hard-fought and ongoing, Janet said. The Gem Theater on Main Street had been triplexed, but at least it was still open. It was showing one film that had the word "fatal" in the title, one with "deadly," and one with "mortal."

I had a town map and an Edensburg phone book with me and had no trouble locating Dick Puderbaugh's fuel-oil distributership. I thought he might be willing to talk with me in a general way about the Osbornes' intrafamily feuding over the future of the *Herald* and I'd pick up an odd, useful nugget on the family dynamics, particularly the propensity among some Osbornes for violence. But as soon as I introduced myself, Puderbaugh, a whey-faced little man with what looked like a rodent insignia on the left breast of his golf shirt, turned hostile.

Puderbaugh fumed that he and June had both been insulted by Janet's "accusation" that a connection existed between Eric's murder and the pro-InfoCom Osbornes. He said it was "a goddamn shame" that people like himself and his wife could have their "private rights" interfered with by people like me. Puderbaugh was barely coherent and bordering on the hysterical as I backed out the door and said, "Have a good one, Dick."

Following Janet's directions, I drove the four miles out of town to Parson Bates's spats museum and pear orchard. I thought I might chat him up too on the split among the Osbornes. Bates was up in a tree when I pulled in, sitting on a branch about eight feet off the ground. I walked up a knoll toward him, and when he recognized me he glowered. Perched up there, Bates looked like a man who might be going to tell me that he had just been taken for a ride by space aliens.

Instead, he yelled down at me, "I do believe I detect a detective— or would I be venturing too far afield in my verbal perambulations if I began again and put it thusly: I do believe I detect a defective." Bates said this with the type of loony-eyed jovial sneer rarely encountered outside state mental institutions prior to the deinstitutionalization consent decrees of the 1960s and '70s. Here was a man you might have expected to be arrested in a midtown Manhattan subway station for sticking his face down the bosoms of young matrons while he whistled "Heartaches," and up here in Edensburg he was considered by many to be a solid citizen. So much for rusticity as an inducement to clear thought.

"Good afternoon, Mr. Bates," I yelled up at him. "I just thought I'd drop by and see if you might give me a few moments of your time. I'm interested in hearing as many points of view as possible on the conflict over the disposition of the *Herald,* and I know you've had a long association with the paper and the Osborne family."

That seemed like an innocuous enough opener, but Bates made no move to climb down and stand on the same ground I stood on. "The disposition of the *Edensburg Herald* is none of your concern," he said, giving me his fish eye. "It is solely the concern of the Osborne family. Not that family life is a subject you would know anything about, I believe I have been reliably informed."

"Oh, I come from a family too, Mr. Bates. And I have observed others. They're all over the place. Anyway, the Osbornes', like all families, is made up of individuals. One of those individuals has been murdered, and attempts have been made on the lives of other Osbornes. Did you know that this morning someone tried to run Dan Osborne's car off a rural road?" A quick glance at Bates's parked Hillman Minx helped eliminate him as a suspect.

"Yes," Bates said testily, "I am aware that Dan drove his car into a ditch earlier today. As for the precise circumstances of the mishap— let's just say that his sister June relayed to me Dan's version of the incident. But it is June's belief, and mine, that dubiety is in order. Item: Dan Osborne is a marijuana addict. Most of the time, he and Arlene Thurber are stuporous. Surely, safe driving is a stranger to the both of them. Item: Dan Osborne can be ruthless and conscienceless on behalf of his causes. In his youth—and I mean his actual youth, not his latter-day infantilism—Dan Osborne was found to have planted an explosive device in the offices of an antiwar organization in an attempt to create the appearance that the FBI was persecuting war protestors. Conclusion: both Dan Osborne's mind and morals are impaired. I would be strongly inclined to await the outcome of a thorough police investigation before I drew any conclusion that this morning's event constituted an actual attempt on Dan's life. A more likely verdict will be trickery."

"I heard the story from both Dan and Arlene," I said, "and whatever

114

their moral and other habits, their version of this morning's incident rings true."

Bates sniffed and said, "I remain unconvinced. You don't know those two. All this talk of murder afoot is nonsense. Eric, poor lost lad, was slain by a homicidal maniac on the loose, according to the State Police. And as for Janet's contention that she was menaced by a Jet Skier, my estimation of the event is that she misperceived the motorized behavior of some doltish and unmannerly youth—suchlike are everywhere these days, heaven knows—and she became unstrung over it. You know how women can be."

One phone call to an old friend of mine active in the Albany chapter of Lesbian Avengers might have further interfered with Bates's lazy afternoon among his pear crop, but I had more pressing concerns. I said, "I was present for one of the Jet Ski attacks, Mr. Bates. In fact, my partner, Timothy Callahan, was injured. His foot was broken when he was hit by the skier. Everyone who witnessed this incident—and there were four of us—agreed that what it was was attempted murder."

"I doubt that very much. In my estimation, you and your cohorts simply saw what suited your agenda."

It was probably his use of "agenda" that did it—the term had come to be used by the loony right more or less interchangeably with "flamethrower"—and the words flew out of my mouth before I could snatch them back. I said, "You're a blithering idiot, Bates."

He shot back, "As of this moment, you are trespassing on my property!"

I reached down, ripped a dandelion leaf out of Bates's meadow, and stuffed it in my mouth. I looked up at him, munching.

Red-faced, Bates stammered, "Begone! Begone!"

I went.

Timmy's Aunt Moira had a favorite piece of advice she gave herself and others when faced with one of life's passing irritants: Get mad; then get over it. It drove Timmy crazy when Aunt Moira came out with this—not because it wasn't often sensible advice, but because he knew she would have said the same thing to Mahatma Gandhi. Parson Bates did not represent one of the major evils of the century, however, as far as I knew, so the scale of my situation with him brought to mind Aunt Moira's generally wise counsel, and I had little trouble abiding by it.

At the Edensburg Country Club, Tidy Puderbaugh wasn't any

happier to see me than his father had been at the fuel-oil office or Parson Bates had been in his tree. A pear-shaped, prematurely jowly, immaculately groomed man of thirty or so in a rep tie and blue blazer, Tidy was in the middle of a bridge game with three young men similarly gotten up. Unlike his father and Parson Bates, however, Tidy appeared unflustered by my unplanned appearance. He said cordially, "My mother's attorney has advised me not to talk to anyone in regards to the *Herald*. As an attorney, I would have given me the same advice." Tidy seemed to think of that as a witticism; he grinned slyly at his bridge partner, who grinned slyly back.

I said, "The conflict over the *Herald* is an incidental part of what I'm looking into. I'm investigating a murder and two or three instances of attempted murder. All the victims and intended victims were members of your family. Could we get together for a few minutes after your game, Attorney Puderbaugh?"

The four bridge players frowned over this, but none lunged at me. They watched their cards serenely. Tidy appeared to be the most placid of all. Whatever the mental idiosyncrasies of his branch of the Osborne clan, attention deficit disorder did not appear to be one of them.

"After this game," Tidy said, "I've got another game scheduled. If you'll call my office and talk to Lillian, she'll set you up for something next week or the week after, over at the office." He fished in a side pocket, came up with a business card, and held it out to me. I accepted the card, considered chewing it up and swallowing it, but stuffed it in my pocket instead.

I said, "If there's an ongoing violent plot to eliminate an anti-InfoCom Osborne from the *Herald* board of directors, next week or the week after might be too late. I was hoping to pick your brain sooner than that on any background or insights you might have that could aid my investigation, however indirectly."

Tidy shrugged lightly and said, "I wouldn't worry about murder plots if I were you, Mr. Strachey. I've heard that's the story you and my Aunt Janet and some other people are spreading around Edensburg. But the only thing you're achieving by spreading this crap around is, you are embarrassing my family."

"I'm trying hard to achieve more than that. But few members of your family are giving me much help."

Tidy peered purposefully at his cards, not at me, and said, "And I'd be surprised if that situation changed anytime soon."

I waited, and when he continued to ignore me, I said to him over his shoulder, "Too bad you're playing bridge, not hearts." Then I left.

Having spent what felt like a useless afternoon getting stonewalled by anti-Griscomb, pro-InfoCom Osbornes and their allies, I was about to head back to Maple Street and report my futile wheel spinning to Timmy, Dale and—if they were back at the house—Janet, Dan, and Arlene.

But when I came to the turnoff for Summit Road, I hung a left, on impulse, and drove up the long hill to Chester and Pauline Osborne's house. As I had hoped, only one shiny Lexus, the teal one, was parked in the cul-de-sac. I left my dusty Mitsubishi next to it, walked over, and rapped on the main door of the big house. The bronze knocker made an impressive racket, but half a minute went by and no one responded. I knocked again and was about to give up, when the door suddenly opened and I was face-to-face with a woman I assumed to be the blonde I'd caught a quick, back-of-the-head glimpse of when I'd called on Chester the night before.

"Yes?"

Like everybody else that afternoon, she wasn't happy to see me. The tension in her narrow tanned face was partly from obvious subcutaneous cantilevering for cosmetic purposes, but the wiring couldn't have been responsible for the fear in her hazel eyes.

"How do you do. I'm Don Strachey. Are you Mrs. Osborne?"

She was dressed in tennis whites, though the object in her hand aimed at me was not a racket but a .38 caliber revolver. In a flat, tight voice, she said, "I'm Pauline Osborne. Are you the detective?"

"I might be, or I might not be. Which is the answer you'd like to hear?"

She didn't chuckle. Not moving, she stared at me for a long moment, apparently trying to decide something about me—Shoot me? Trust me? Ask me in for a drink?—or about something or someone else. Her eyes were full of indecision and pain and—even though my manner was unthreatening—fear.

Finally, she said, "You are the detective. I saw your car last night when you came here to see my husband."

I said, "It sounds like you've been doing some detective work yourself, Mrs. Osborne." She flinched when I said this, and I quickly added,

"But I am the private investigator from Albany you might have heard about. I've been retained by Janet to investigate Eric's death and attempts on the lives of two other Osbornes, Janet and Dan."

"Dan too?" she said, and her eyes widened.

"This morning someone tried to run his car off the road. Arlene Thurber was riding with him, and they barely avoided being shoved over a cliff. The State Police are investigating too. I'm surprised the police haven't been up to see you already."

This startled her, and I said, "Would you mind pointing that gun somewhere else? I'm harmless, and if you inadvertently blew bits and pieces of me all over that fine automobile of yours, it could badly interfere with your tennis schedule."

She looked down at the .38 for the first time, shuddered, lowered it, then looked back at me. Suddenly, Pauline Osborne shrieked at the top of her lungs. Her face twisted with rage, and I hoped nothing inside it snapped. Then she slammed the door in my face. She shrieked again, then, some seconds later, a third time. I listened for a gunshot and thought about smashing my way into the house. But I waited, and after five or ten minutes went by, I got into my car and drove away. In those five or ten minutes, there had been no gunshot, just the occasional shriek from somewhere deep inside Chester and Pauline Osborne's house. A half mile down the hill, I thought I heard still another shriek, but that one I probably imagined.

17

Friday morning I hit the road early for the three-hour drive out to Attica. I had the radio on for a while, but the news on *Morning Edition* was unrelievedly bad—tornadoes, Bosnia, Newt—so I shoved a Betty Carter tape into the player. Some of her news was bad too, but with a musical ingenuity that seemed to rival the engineering feats of Leonardo, Carter transformed both good and bad news into the aural equivalent of human flight. The miles flew by, and I would have enjoyed the solitary couple of hours of sublime music while cruising under a deep, cloudless August sky, except for the fact that as I drove I was nagged by two events of the day before.

One was Pauline Osborne's greeting me at the entrance to her home with a pistol, followed by her sudden, unprompted screams of what I took to be rage and frustration. A few hours afterward, I had described this scene to Janet, Dale, Timmy, Dan, and Arlene. None of them knew what to make of it. Janet said Pauline had long been prone to both anxiety and depression and probably relied a little too heavily on alcohol to get from one shopping day to the next. But Pauline had never shown signs of a crack-up coming on, nor had she brandished a firearm, as far as anyone present knew. So what did this incident mean?

The other disconcerting revelation of that evening concerned Craig Osborne. I had asked Janet for tear sheets or printouts from the *Herald* library on the jewel heist that had landed Craig in prison. She had brought them back to the house, and I read them and discussed the clippings with members of our odd, jittery household while an Edensburg policeman watched over us from his cruiser parked across Maple Street.

Osborne, I learned, had been tried and convicted the previous November of robbing a luxury hotel in Tarrytown, Westchester County, New York. A second armed robber, who turned out to be a part-time hotel employee, had been shot and killed by a hotel security guard during the middle-of-the-night stickup. Craig had escaped, for a time, with the loot—a box of high-quality cut diamonds and other gems. The jewels had been stored in a hotel vault overnight and were owned by a party of hotel guests, a wealthy Kuwaiti family in the area for a wedding the next day in nearby Briarcliff Manor.

Craig had shot and killed the security guard before making his escape, and that was one reason for his long prison term, twenty-five years to life. The other reason for the trial judge's imposition of the maximum sentence for Osborne was this: When Craig was captured three days after the robbery—he had been wounded in the leg in the shoot-out and a suspicious nurse at an Oneonta walk-in clinic alerted the police—the gun Craig had used in the robbery was still with him, stashed in his luggage in a motel room. But the stolen jewels were nowhere to be found.

At the time, none of the Osbornes had thought much about the missing jewels. They were busy coping with their shock over Chester and Pauline's only son having committed a horrible violent crime. The armed robbery itself was uppermost in the minds of everyone in the family, and the police and the hotel's insurers would have to worry about the jewels. Craig had repeatedly insisted to the police that he had dropped the box of gems outside the hotel in his panicked getaway. While this was considered possible—a dishonest passerby might have picked the jewels up and made off with them—a likelier scenario, according to police, was that Craig had either handed the jewels off to a third accomplice, or he had hid them in anticipation of his eventual release from prison or even a possible escape.

The Osbornes I spoke with on Maple Street that evening said they had failed to make anything of the fact, or even notice, that the estimated value of the missing jewels from the Tarrytown robbery was nearly the same amount—$16 million—as the *Herald* company debt that had forced the Osbornes to put the paper up for sale. When I pointed this out, Janet said it struck her as a kind of goofy coincidence and she urged me not to head off on an unpromising tangent. She said that if Craig had meant for the proceeds of the robbery to erase the

Herald's debt, he'd have planned some elaborate fencing and money-laundering scheme—Craig was violent and amoral but not stupid, Janet said—and the money would have turned up already and saved the *Herald*. Dale, Timmy, Arlene, and I began to speculate on ways that the jewels or cash might have somehow gotten waylaid or diverted from their intended purpose. That's when Dan excused himself again and headed for the bathroom.

"I was wondering how long it was gonna take before somebody with some smarts came along and made the connection," Craig Osborne said. "We didn't even know the fucking jewels were *worth* sixteen million. We figured we'd have to make two hits, or five, or a hundred, before we had a stash big enough to pay that fucking bank what the *Herald* owed it. We about shit when we hit the fucking big payoff on the first hit."

"You said 'we,' Craig. You and who else?"

"Me and cousin Dan," he said, giving me a big Jack Nicholson-style demonic grin. "Who the fuck else do you think it could've been?"

Craig Osborne was a tall, rangy, bony-faced man with long, thinning straw-colored hair, cool gray eyes, a cold sore above his upper lip, and a fresh bruise on his left temple. The Plexiglas divider between us was filthy and smudged, as if Osborne's last visitor had been his pet rottweiler, and this made it harder to read his face and eyes. There was also the sobering reality that among the Osborne family, Craig was famous as a liar. Yet my inclination was to believe him. I had barely introduced myself when Osborne began to vent. He warned me that he would refuse to repeat anything he was telling me to the police or to the prosecutors, and he would deny to them that he had talked to me about anything other than the American League pennant race. Yet here he was spilling his guts to a stranger, and he was confirming my suspicions that Dan-of-the-sensitive-stomach was deeply involved in— what? It looked like some wild and woolly attempt to save the *Herald* through illegal means that had somehow gone all wrong.

I said, "Why are you telling me this, Craig? You don't even know me."

"I know enough about you," he said cockily, "to know that you are the man I need to talk to."

"And what is it that you know about me?"

Osborne laid his sinewy forearms on the table and leaned closer to the glass. He said, "Dan called me up yesterday and told me about this hot-shit private eye called Strachey. He said you'd been hired by my cousin Janet and Eldon McCaslin to find out who killed Eric. Dan said if you came out here, I should tell you to fuck off because if I told you anything I'd just get the law after him, and that wouldn't do anybody any good and it wouldn't help the *Herald*. But as you can tell," he said with a sneer, "I'm telling you everything I know about the deep shit the Osbornes are in. I mean *everything*."

"Okay."

"You are one lucky dick, Strachey."

"Uh-huh."

The sneer faded, and he said coolly, "There are a couple of small things I want from you in return. One of them is easy."

"What's that?"

He looked at me and said, "I want you to find out where the jewels are. I want you to report this information to me."

I said nothing.

He went on. "I don't need them. I sure as fuck don't have any use for diamonds in this house of scumbags. I just want to know. I'm curious. Artie would have been interested too."

"Who is Artie?"

"Artie Wozniak. Artie was blown away in the hit at the hotel. Artie got killed for nothing. That sucks. I want you to tell me why Artie got killed for shit." He watched me expressionlessly.

I said, "Where does Dan say the jewels are? Or wasn't he the third accomplice who ended up with the jewels?"

"Dan got the jewels, sure. The hit was his idea too. He always knew I was a fucking thief. Everybody in Edensburg knew that. It was Dan's idea that I could use my talent for being an asshole for a good cause. And when we made the hit, Dan was down the road from the hotel. I made the handoff to Dan, and then I drove up to Oswego with my leg ripped open, and this hot-looking nurse turned me in. Dan was supposed to stash the jewels in Edensburg somewhere until this Cuban he knew came through—some kahuna with the Cuban U.N. office—and this guy would be the fence in return for a cut. But something went wrong. Fucking Dan won't tell me what it was, but he's trying to fix it, so he says. He says the fucking jewels got away from him, and he's busting his balls, he keeps telling me, to get them back. He says to me he's embarrassed. Embarrassed! Embarrassed, shit. I want to know where those fucking jewels went. I deserve to know."

"I suppose you do."

"And if you're working for Janet," Osborne said casually, "you can help Dan find the jewels, and you can still use them to keep the fucking *Herald* from being taken over by assholes like Chester Osborne."

This was getting treacherous. I said, "I couldn't do that. If I found the jewels, I'd have to return them to the police, or the gems' owners, or their insurance company. That's a given. I have no choice."

He gave me a look—one of the two or three in his repertory—that bordered on the salacious, except it had to do with an appetite other than sex. He said, "You could do it. And you will too." Then his face hardened. "Have you met my father?"

"Yes, I have."

"Do you want that piece of shit to control the future of the *Herald?*" He waited.

"No," I said.

"Then the jewels have to be used."

"Even if the *Herald's* debt isn't paid off by the September deadline," I said, "a majority of the company's board members are planning to sell the *Herald* to Harry Griscomb, who'll retain the paper's staff and standards and probably keep Janet on to run it. Your father is one of a minority on the board who want to sell out to a sleazy bottom-line-oriented chain, but it looks as if this can be kept from happening. So your father is not going to control the future of the *Herald,* no matter where the jewels end up. I know you aren't crazy about your father, Craig, and I think I know some of the reasons why you don't want to see him get his way. But even without the jewels, your father won't succeed. Janet is determined to keep it from happening."

Osborne sneered. "You don't fucking get it."

"Get what?"

He slowly shook his head. "Dan told me somebody tried to hit him with a truck and drown Janet with a Jet Ski. You really don't get what's happening here?"

"It's true that attempts have been made on Janet's and Dan's lives. And all the indications are that these attacks are meant to knock Dan and Janet off the *Herald's* board. Yes, I get that. But Janet and Dan are both under police protection now. So is your grandmother. We can keep them safe until after the board votes on September eighth, and that's what we're going to do. The stolen jewels, Craig, are irrelevant now. Sorry."

"The fuck you can protect them," Osborne said. "Chester Osborne will find a way to get to one of them—Dan or Janet or Grandma—just like he killed my cousin Eric." Again he watched me with his unreadable eyes, the eyes of a habitual liar, the other Osbornes said.

"Your father killed Eric? How do you know that?"

"He told me."

"Uh-huh."

"In December, my father came out here and talked to me for the first time in ten years. When the warden told me Chester was up here, I wanted to come up here and stick a fork in his gut. But I figured I'd never get close enough to him to do it. Then I thought, fuck it, I'm not even gonna come up here and look at his stupid face. But then I thought, maybe I can come up here and find out something I can use against him. So I came."

"Right."

"I came up here and I actually talked to old shitface. And what he wanted was, he knew Dan had been trying to track me down before the hotel hit. Then when the jewels weren't recovered after I was picked up, Chester put two and two together and came up with this idea that was basically what had happened. I guess Chester's where I got my criminal mind from. He told me if Dan or I used the take from the hit to save the *Herald,* he would see that an investigation happened and Dan would be fucked.

"And then the evil old man—you'll love this—then old Chester Osborne demands that he get control over the sixteen million. Dan's Cuban had set up a plan to have the jewels fenced in Venezuela and then have the cash funneled through a bank in the Caymans. Chester had a bank in the Bahamas we were supposed to use—the cash was supposed to come back in the form of a loan to the *Herald* from this bank, supposedly, only the terms of the loan would be so easy that it was like the *Herald* never really had to pay it back. The loan deal was all just cover.

"The one part of the Bahamas loan agreement that Chester liked the most was, the loan would only go through if Janet, Eric, and Dan all got off the *Herald* board, and Tidy and two people from outside the family came on the board, and Stu Torkildson would be the publisher." Osborne smiled mirthlessly. "So you tell me, Mr. Private Dick? Where do I get my criminal tendencies from? Huh?"

I said, "I see your point. So, did you agree to your father's criminal demands, Craig?"

Looking smug, Osborne said, "I told him he was full of shit and I blew him off. I'd love to have told him the truth. But then Chester would've gone after Dan too soon, and that could've blown the whole deal. I warned Dan that Chester was suspicious and to make sure the source of the Cayman loan couldn't be traced. Dan said the Cuban said it was foolproof, so then I dropped the subject. I figured I'd have to get my satisfaction just from knowing that Chester wasn't getting control of the *Herald*—that he'd gotten fucked over, even if I couldn't rub his ugly face in it."

I said, "But that wasn't the end of it with your father, I guess."

He shook his head. "Fuck, no."

"He came back out here again?"

"In May," Osborne said. "A week before Eric was killed."

"What did your father want this time?"

"When the jewels still didn't turn up," Osborne said, looking me directly in the eye, as he had since my arrival, "old Chester starts thinking that Dan and Eric and I did do the job, and Dan and Eric have got some kind of last-minute surprise that will squeeze Chester and Stu Torkildson out of the *Herald* totally. That's how good a judge of people my father is—he thought my straight cousin Eric was in on the hit! Eric was queer, but he was still the straightest guy I ever knew—nuts and berries and grass and trees and all that shit that's supposed to turn Osbornes on, though as for me, you can have it.

"So Chester comes out here in May, and he's ripshit. He says he knows something is up, and where the fuck are the jewels? By then, though, see, Dan has told me the fucking jewels are missing. That's what Dan says—they're missing and he's trying to locate them, he says. Since I want to know where the fuck the fucking jewels are myself, I tell Chester, ask Dan where they are. And this is just what Chester needs to hear. It was a fucking dumb thing for me to say—Eric might still be alive if I'd kept my mouth shut—but I was pissed at Dan by then, and at everybody else, and I just didn't give a fuck."

"So your father went back and confronted Dan?"

Osborne snorted. "Dan told him to fuck off. Dan denied everthing. He said I was playing head games with Chester to get even with him for how he treated me when I was a kid."

"How did he treat you?" I said.

Osborne looked at me with his dead eyes and said, "My father beat the shit out of me every chance he got. He'd do it when my mother wasn't around. Whenever we were alone, he'd pound on me. My mother knew it, but she ignored it." He watched me with his blank look.

I said, "I can see why you want revenge."

"That's what I want."

"You're getting it at a high price. It looks as if your life is your revenge."

Now he looked irritated. "Who the fuck are you, Adolph Freud? Hey, shit, man, do you think I'm too stupid to understand that? Fuck yes, my life is my revenge against my father."

I said, "You could have waited until you were bigger than your father and then punched his face in. That's crude and illegal, but people in your situation do it and it sometimes seems to make a difference."

He said, "I'm not a patient person."

"What happened," I asked, "after Dan told your father he was mistaken in his suspicions?"

"My father went to Eric."

"How do you know he did?"

"Dan told me. Eric called Dan one day, Dan told me, and said Chester had been running at the mouth with Eric about some jewel robbery, and asking where were the fucking jewels, and Eric asked Dan what the fuck Chester was talking about. Dan told Eric that this was just some shit I had made up to fuck up my father's head. Then Eric went back to Chester to tell him there was nothing to the jewel-hit story, and my father had one of his violent fits that he has, and killed him."

I watched Osborne and waited, but he just sat there looking at me as if we were discussing the General Agreement on Tariffs and Trade and it was my turn to add a pertinent thought.

I said, "You're saying that your father killed Eric impulsively, in a rage of frustration, after Eric—what? Disappointed him by refusing to confess about the sixteen-million-dollar jewel heist that your father was convinced Eric was involved in?"

126

"That's what set him off," Osborne said. "Chester has been famous since he was a kid for beating on people. You must have heard about that from Janet. She knows the story." I nodded. "So," Osborne said, "old Chester finally beat somebody to death. Too bad for Eric."

I said, "And your father admitted this to you?"

"In so many words, he did."

"What were those words?"

"He told me on the phone a week after Eric was offed that Eric deserved what he got for trying to screw Chester and June by hogging all the credit for saving the *Herald* with the jewel heist. Chester was still convinced Dan was about to spring something, even though by then Dan had lost control of the jewels. My father also said Eric deserved what he got because Eric was trying to keep the *Herald* under the control of hippies and socialists, and Chester said their day was past."

I said, "That's a powerful expression of sentiment on your father's part, but it's not an admission of guilt."

"It's as much of an admission as I need," Osborne said laconically. "I know my father. That's the other fucking reason I'm telling you this, as a matter of fact. I can't tell all this to the prosecutors or they'll go after Dan. I don't want that—at least not yet. It depends on what my radical cousin did with the jewels. If he gave the jewels to some fucking coffee-pickers' liberation front somewhere—which he has been known to do with Osborne family money—I am going to be extremely pissed off. But I'll wait to hear about that. While you're on Janet's tit, you can go ahead and clear it up for me as to just what became of the goddamn jewels. And the other thing you can do for me, Strachey, is you can fucking nail Chester Osborne for Eric's murder. That's what you can do for me and for the entire human race."

I sat looking at him and wondering how much of what Osborne had told me was true, how much of it lies, how much of it fantasy fed by his boiling need for revenge.

I said, "Have you told anyone else, Craig, the story you've told me here this morning?"

He said, "Just my mother. I called her up on Wednesday and told her there were some things about her husband I thought she needed to know."

18

Back in Edensburg just after four, I drove directly to Ruth Osborne's house. Now that I had the goods—or what I confidently believed closely resembled the goods—on Dan, I was eager to confront him.

"He's gone," Timmy said. "Arlene too."

"They left a note," Dale said. "It just said 'Don't worry about us.' But they didn't say where they went or when they'd be back."

Timmy and Dale were seated across from each other at the dinner table on the back porch. I could hear Elsie moving about in the kitchen nearby, and Ruth Osborne was outside, fifty feet away, snipping something with a scissors into a basket in the herb garden. Timmy and Dale were in the midst of a game of Scrabble and acted distracted and vaguely annoyed by my interruption.

"When did they leave?" I asked.

"It must have been not long after you did," Timmy said. "We were all still asleep. What time did you leave for Attica?"

"Six-thirty."

"I was up at seven," Dale said, "and they were out of here by then. They left the note here on the table."

"Would you like some iced tea?" Timmy asked, indicating a perspiring crystal pitcher and a tray of glasses.

Helping myself, I said, "Where's the note?"

It appeared to be Dale's turn in the Scrabble game, so it was Timmy who glanced around the room in search of Dan's note. "Here it is." He turned over the sheet of typing paper their Scrabble scores were written on—Dale was leading, 180 to 167—and on the other side was the scrawled note: "Don't worry about us—Dan."

I said, "Is that Dan's handwriting?"

"I think so," Dale said, not looking up from her letter holder. "Janet saw it, and she didn't say it *wasn't* Dan's handwriting."

"Did the phone ring, that anybody knows of, before they left? Could they have received a call from someone?"

"I didn't hear it," Timmy said. "And there's a phone in our room."

"Ours too," Dale said. "But it's only rung once all day. That was around noon, when Pauline called for Janet."

"Was Janet here?"

"Yes, she came home for lunch," Timmy said. Now both Dale and Timmy were furiously rearranging the letter squares on their holders.

"Did Janet say why Pauline called her?"

Dale ignored this, and Timmy shook his head and said, "Nnn-nnn."

"Janet didn't say anything about Pauline still being upset after the way she held a gun on me yesterday?"

"Nnn-nnn."

Leaning against a nearby wicker settee were Timmy's wooden crutches, and my impulse was to pick one of them up and sweep all the letter squares off the Scrabble board and onto the players' laps. Instead, I said, "Aren't you two curious to hear about my meeting with Craig out at Attica? It was eventful."

Not looking up, Timmy said, "Absolutely."

"Yes, Donald," Dale said, "but if you don't mind keeping your dick in your pants until we're through with this game, that'll be just too, too groovy."

I picked up one of the crutches, played with it, put it back.

"It might look as if we've got our priorities screwed up," Timmy said, "but this game is more important than it may seem. Each word that Dale places on the board is meant to offer a clue about what it is I once did that makes me a moral slug in her eyes."

"And each word that Timmy plays shows his reaction to the word I last played," Dale said.

I studied the board. Among the words snaking this way and that way, up and down the board, were these: FIB, ILL, LIAR, RETCH, CUFFED, DUCKY, CURT, UMBRAGE, KNEED, EEL, DORKY, RIPRAP.

I said, "Is 'riprap' a clue or a response?"

"Neither, exactly," Timmy said. "But it got me a triple-letter score. That was the response I felt like expressing at the time."

"Which was not following the agreed-upon rules of the game," Dale said. "When he played that word, Timothy was not keeping his word—as usual."

Timmy frowned deeply as Dale spelled out "pimp."

I left them and walked outside across the broad back lawn, aromatic and abuzz with bees, to the herb garden. Ruth Osborne had placed a low flat basket on the ground beside the spot where she was bending over. The basket contained eight perfect sun-ripened tomatoes that must have come from the vegetable garden in the southeast corner of the yard. Mrs. Osborne had snipped off a small bunch of basil sprigs, and their perfume in the heat of the late afternoon was strong and transporting. Scientists who know the geography of the human brain say the olfactory and memory centers are located next to each other, and that's why smells can trigger such powerful memories. Basil set off a welter of memories for me, all of them good. Among them were my grandmother's vegetable garden in Phillipsburg, New Jersey, and beside her herb patch a hidden pathway through the brush down to the banks of the Delaware River. Then it was on to lunches with Timmy at our *pensione* in Fiesoli, and on and on in a fraction of a second.

"Smells wonderful," I said.

Mrs. Osborne straightened up slowly and said, "This is the season I'll miss when I'm dead. It isn't even a season—just a week or two in August when the tomatoes are at their peak and the basil hasn't begun to wilt and the local corn is sweetest. What luck it is for a person to be up and around and conscious in Edensburg in August!"

I said, "It's one of the times of the year when we remember why we live in this part of the country."

"Oh, I live in Edensburg because I came back here and married Tom Osborne," she said, "instead of marrying one of the boys from Yale who came up to Mount Holyoke on weekends. If I'd married Ogden Winsted of Philadelphia, I'd have gone off with him to darkest Chestnut Hill and never been heard of again. Or if I'd accepted Lew McAlister's proposal of marriage, I'd probably still be in the Cameroons shining Christ's light on the heathen. Either locale would have left me a long way from Edensburg.

"There were other offers, too, some of them worth considering. But

I loved Tom Osborne from the time he was a sixth-grade . . . 'patrol boy' was what the school crossing guards were called back then, and I was a frightened first grader, and Tom held my hand every day when I crossed Third Street on the way to Stuyvesant Grammar.

"I adored Tom and felt safe and secure with him, and although much later, of course, I had to set him straight on a few matters—he could be dumb as a post when it came to what he used to call 'the female of the species'—still, I never in all our fifty-nine years together stopped leaning on Tom or looking up to him. You know, Mr. Donaldson, I was just thinking: Tom had asked that his ashes be scattered in the mountains, and I was too selfish to let the kids do that. Even though Tom is now just bits and pieces of bone and whatnot, I drew comfort from having what's left of him around. But now I've come up with another idea. Why not spread Tom's remains around in the herb garden? That way he'd be out in the weather, which is what he wanted. At the same time, I could visit him—and I do use that term loosely—and I could continue to be reassured by Tom's nearby presence, however irrational that may seem to others. What do you think?"

I said, "I don't know. Is that legal?"

"Oh, do you suppose it might not be?"

"Just to be on the safe side, maybe you should consult an attorney, Mrs. Osborne. And an agronomist."

"I suppose I ought to."

"As a precaution."

"You don't hear of people," she said, "being hauled into court for—what would the charge be? If it's on your own property it wouldn't be littering. And I don't believe there's any hazard to public health—the cremation fire surely would eliminate any risk of bacteriological contamination. What would any legal objection possibly be based on?"

She had me there. I said, "It won't hurt to ask. You might learn something neither of us knew."

She looked doubtful and unconvinced. "It's nothing I need to worry about today," she said. "Today we've all got more immediate concerns. How is your investigation progressing, Mr. Donaldson? Have you accumulated enough evidence yet to have Chester charged with fratricide?"

"I am making progress, Mrs. Osborne, but I'm still short on any evidence a prosecutor could use in making a case that would stand up in court. As for Chester's being a murderer, I don't know about that."

"Well, I sure as the devil know about it. Just you keep digging, and it's Chester you'll get the goods on. I know my son." This was said not with irony, so far as I could tell, but with some weird combination of clinical detachment and maternal conviction.

I said, "Chester has a reputation for violent explosions of temper, Mrs. Osborne, but has he ever been calculating in his violent acts? As far as I've been able to determine, premeditation doesn't seem to be his style."

"He was always sly," she said thoughtfully. "And I hate to say it, but frequently untruthful too."

"Scheming in business, or even family matters, is one thing," I said. "But my question to you is, on those occasions in his life when Chester actually hurt people, did it ever seem planned?"

"No, it always seemed to erupt out of nowhere. And I'm sure, Mr. Samuelson, that when you get to the bottom of it, you'll find that that's what happened with Chester and Eric. Eric refused to change his vote on selling the *Herald* to Harry Griscomb, and then Chester blew up at Eric, and this time he murdered him." She looked pained but not horrified, as if fratricide were a difficult matter that the Osbornes had to contend with, the way another family might have to face a child born out of wedlock or a scandal involving the personal use of PTA funds.

"But why," I asked, "would Chester and Eric be discussing *Herald* business affairs on a hiking trail miles from town? Is Chester a hiker?"

"Sometimes he used to be," she said. "All the Osbornes are naturalists. Even June was as a child."

"Did Eric and Chester go hiking together—in recent years, as adults?"

"I wouldn't think so. I'd be awfully surprised."

I said, "You're not the only member of your family, Mrs. Osborne, who believes that Chester murdered Eric. But the more I think about it, the more trouble I have imagining the two of them meeting in the woods by chance and an argument ensuing during which Chester loses control and bludgeons Eric, who dies. Nor can I imagine Chester the hothead plotting to follow Eric nearly a mile into the woods, where he sneaks up on Eric and pounds him with a weapon he's carried along from home. Both are out of character. Either is possible, but I think unlikely."

Mrs. Osborne was due in court in three days to answer a charge of having gone soft in the head, but on that Friday afternoon in her herb garden she looked alert and her reactions to what I told her suggested full comprehension—even though she couldn't seem to get my name right. She said, "But why else would Chester say what he said to me about somebody else having to get hurt in order to keep the *Herald* out of Harry Griscomb's hands?"

"It's possible," I said, "that this was just Chester blowing off steam—losing his temper with you and blurting out something he knew would hurt you and frighten you. Doing that would be in character for Chester."

Looking bewildered, she said, "Then you don't think it's Chester who's plotting to change the makeup of the *Herald* board and prevent the sale to Harry Griscomb?"

I told her I was not prepared to absolve Chester of anything—maybe not even Eric's murder—but that I thought a broader, more complex conspiracy was under way. I said I believed some members of the conspiracy were unaware of the activities of other members of the conspiracy, and that it was probable only one or possibly two conspirators were behind Eric's murder and the more recent attempts on Janet's and Dan's lives. Without mentioning Craig Osborne and the diamond robbery and Dan's alleged criminal activities on behalf of saving the *Herald,* I told Mrs. Osborne that she should be prepared in the coming days for a number of revelations about Osborne family members that might shock and disappoint her.

She listened with interest to all of this, and said, "You've got quite a lurid imagination, Mr. Donaldson. My curiosity is certainly piqued. But I've found that the truest answers to hard questions tend to be the simplest ones. I hope you aren't being led astray by the fact that most of us Osbornes are, to one extent or another, nuts. It would be a pity if you were thrown off by Osborne looniness."

I asked her which Osbornes were the loony ones I should be careful not to be misled by, and she had a good laugh over that.

19

Ruth Osborne said she had no idea where Dan and Arlene might have gone off to, and when Janet arrived at the house an hour later, she said she too was baffled. There was no indication Dan and Arlene had been lured into a trap, yet they had been gone for more than ten hours without letting anyone know of their whereabouts. Janet phoned all of Dan and Arlene's friends in the immediate area that she could think of, but none said they had heard from Dan and Arlene. One—or all—of them could have been lying, but we had no way of checking.

"What about Liver Livingston?" Dale said. The four of us were having a beer on the back porch. Elsie had left for the day, and Mrs. Osborne had gone into her late husband's study to commune with his cremated remains.

"It seems odd," Timmy said, "that Dan would go visit his dope dealer with the police so interested in his whereabouts. Why would he chance drawing attention to Liver and his illicit enterprise?"

" 'Illicit,' " Dale said. "There's a funny old word."

Janet said, "It won't hurt to check with Liver. I'll see if he's in the phone book. And then, Don, I want to hear about your visit with Craig today. I take it there's no earth-shattering news out of Attica, or we would have been let in on it by now."

Timmy and Dale had finished up their Scrabble game just minutes before—Timmy had scored highest but he still had not puzzled out how he had incurred Dale's wrath some years earlier—and now Timmy said, "Yes, Dale and I are eager to hear about your trip too, Don."

"Cough it up, Donald," Dale said.

Janet had located the Livingstons in the phone book and said, "No Liver Livingston—or Samuel, his real name. There's a Malcolm, and a Robert. Maybe it's one of those two. I'll check." She dialed one number and said, "Have I reached the Liver Livingston residence? No, sorry, wrong number." Then the second number: "Liver Livingston? No, sorry, wrong number."

"Try information," Dale said. "Maybe Liver is unlisted."

Timmy said, "NYNEX doesn't call them 'unlisted' numbers anymore. Now they're called 'nonpublished.' "

"That's quite an advance for Western civilization," Dale said.

Janet asked, "directory assistance"—formerly called "information," and now another phone company innovative piling-on of useless syllables—for Liver or Samuel Livingston's number, but the operator had no data on either, published or otherwise.

"I'm wondering if we should notify the police," Janet said, "if Dan and Arlene aren't back by a certain hour. What do you think?"

I said I thought not yet. I reminded them that Dan had said in his note not to worry about him and Arlene. I said I believed Dan's disappearance might conceivably have devolved from certain complexities in the current situation that up until that moment Janet, Dale, and Timmy had not been privy to. Then I told them about the jewel heist and Dan's criminal complicity.

They looked at me.

Dale said, "Donald, are you shitting us?"

"No."

"A jewel thief!" Timmy said. "Holy mother! Do you believe it, Don?"

Janet had gone white, and now she said, "I can almost believe it."

"Almost?" Dale said.

"I mean, I believe it. I mean, on the one hand I believe it, and yet on the other hand—Craig is probably the biggest pathological liar the family ever produced. So you have to take that into consideration."

I said, "Why might Craig make up a story like that about Dan?"

Janet thought this over. "I don't know," she said finally. "There was never any bad feeling between them that I'm aware of. They never had a whole lot to do with each other, but I don't think Craig ever particularly disliked Dan, either. They just lived very different, separate lives—Dan the political and social rebel, Craig the antisocial mischief maker and eventual criminal. It's possible, I suppose, that Craig harbored some terrible resentment against Dan for being the type of rebel that American society reserves a small, grudging place for that isn't jail. But that's just a guess. Anyway, Craig's story that Dan was in on the robbery—even that the idea for the robbery was Dan's—that part of it rings all too true. Dan always believed that a moral end justified immoral means. It's a point we always disagreed on. Back in the movement days, Dan did some things he admitted to me that would have landed him in federal prison if he'd ever gotten caught. That's all I'm going to say on that subject, but I think you get my point."

We all said we got it.

"But then, where are the stolen jewels?" Janet asked. "Dan told Craig they 'got away' from him? What does that mean?"

"That's what I planned on asking Dan, but it seems I can't, because he's gone. My guess is, Dan was afraid Craig might be going to tell me about Dan's involvement in the robbery, and that's one reason he bolted minutes after I left for Attica."

"And maybe the other reason he left," Dale said, "was to try again to locate and retrieve the jewels."

I said I guessed that was the case too.

"Jesus," Janet said, and took a long swig of beer.

"This is just too friggin' much," Dale said.

I said, "And there's more."

They gawked at each other as I repeated Craig's theory—his gut conviction—that after Chester Osborne had learned of the plot to save the *Herald* with the jewel-robbery proceeds, he wrongly accused Eric of participating in the scam and then killed Eric when Eric refused to substitute Chester's fence for Dan's and allow Chester to use the sixteen million to gain control of the *Herald* for Chester, June, and Stu Torkildson.

Both Timmy and Dale were gape-jawed, but Janet said flatly, "There's something wrong with that."

"I think so too," I said.

"I can't believe Chester would ever think Eric was involved in a robbery where two people were killed. Chester knew how straight Eric was. He'd believe it of Dan, but not of Eric."

"On the other hand," Timmy said, "Chester is the brother with the history of violence, not Dan."

"On the third hand," Dale said, "it's Dan who pukes his guts out whenever the subject of Eric's murder comes up. Chester doesn't do that—or does he?"

"Not in my experience," Janet said.

I said, "Nor mine. It's possible, though, that Dan retches at the mention of Eric's murder not because he committed the murder, but because he knows who did. He can't announce to anyone that he knows who did it because the murder was somehow connected to the save-the-*Herald*-with-a-jewel-heist conspiracy, and Dan can't talk about that without risking exposure of his complicity in a crime where an innocent security guard died. Dan is surely grown-up enough now to understand that no cause justifies the murder of an innocent. I suppose he's also sickened by the thought that both the guard and Craig's accomplice in the stickup died uselessly, as far as Dan is concerned. The jewels got away from him somehow—he lost them or they were stolen from him in some kind of double cross or whatever—and the jewels haven't been used by anybody to save the *Herald* from either the good chain or the bad chain."

Timmy said, "That makes sense, but if Dan does know who killed Eric, why couldn't it have been Chester? It might not have been rational for Chester to accuse Eric of being involved in the robbery, but Chester sounds to me like a man with an irrational streak a mile wide."

I asked Janet: "Where were the various members of the Osborne family on the day of Eric's murder? Has this ever been determined? Where were Dan, Chester, June? Where was Tidy? Tacker, we assume, was on an island in the South Pacific, but I'm checking on that. How about Stu Torkildson? He's not family, but he's got a direct interest in the disposition of the *Herald*. Where was Arlene? Or Pauline? Where was your mother? Where was Dale? Where were you?"

Janet said, "The police never questioned all of us. There seemed to be no point in doing so at the time. Some of those people can certainly be ruled out on the grounds that they'd never walk more than ten feet into the wilderness. Pauline, for example. Incidentally, she called me today, and she was looking for Dan too. She said she had to talk to him about something, but she wouldn't say what. She sounded as if she'd had a few drinks, but she wasn't hysterical and didn't sound as if she might be waving a gun around."

"Craig told me today he'd phoned his mother on Wednesday," I said, "and informed her that Chester had killed Eric for not turning over the stolen diamonds. My guess is, that's why Pauline was unhinged when I stopped by her house yesterday. What are the chances she would have believed Craig's malicious story?"

Janet looked deeply skeptical. "Pauline knows better than anyone what a liar Craig is, and how much he despises Chester. Although, even if she didn't believe it, the story is so ugly it could have set Pauline off."

Dale said, "Maybe Pauline is trying to reach Dan to check out the jewel-heist story with him."

"Right," Timmy said. "Maybe she asked Chester about it, and she knows him well enough to have been unconvinced by his denial."

I said I would talk to Pauline Osborne at the first opportunity. Without bringing up Craig's inflammatory phone call, I said, I could approach Pauline under the guise of interviewing all the Osbornes regarding their whereabouts on the morning of Eric's murder. Each Osborne would take umbrage, but none could claim to have been singled out. I said, "In the next forty-eight hours I'll try to get a fix on where each Osborne was at the moment Eric was killed. I'll check on each family member, and Stu Torkildson, and—who else is there? Have I left anybody out?"

"Skeeter," Dale said. "He's actually family too, if your list is going to be inclusive."

Timmy said, "Skeeter? That's absurd."

"The State Police checked his alibi," I said. "Skeeter was in Watertown all day on May fifteenth."

"Yes, they would do that," Dale sneered. "Homophobic twits."

Timmy started to speak, hesitated, looked wary, then opened his mouth anyway. "The idea of Skeeter as a murderer is ridiculous, but generally it is not necessarily homophobic when a gay man is murdered to check his lover's alibi. When a straight woman in this country is murdered, nearly half the time it's her husband, ex-husband, or boyfriend who did it."

Dale looked surprised and said, "You're quite right in your statistical observation, Timothy. It's also true that in most jurisdictions I'm familiar with, when a homosexual man is murdered, the police immediately assume the crime was committed by another homosexual because they can't imagine a straight man wanting any physical contact whatsoever with a gay man, even for purposes of homicide."

She looked at Timmy drolly—I wasn't always certain when Dale was putting him on and when she was hectoring him sincerely—and Timmy said, "That's the biggest load of psychobabble horseshit you've dumped over me since we first met, Dale. I'm speechless."

A faint smile flickered on Dale's lips, then disappeared. "Speechless again, Timothy? Where have I heard that before?"

Timmy screwed up his face and stared at Dale, who stared back, tight-lipped.

Janet said, "I'm not at all that surprised that the police checked Skeeter's alibi for the day Eric was killed—that is routine stuff. But they didn't check out any other Osborne that I'm aware of. I'm trying to remember where everybody was. It happened on a Monday, and I was in the office all day. The murder took place in the morning, the police said. But Eric's body had been dragged off the trail and wasn't discovered by another hiker until late afternoon. And by the time the police notified me it was after five, maybe even closer to six. I know I was just getting ready to leave the *Herald*. I went right to Mom's house and told her—the very, very worst thing I have ever had to do.

"The cops asked me to notify June, Dan, and Chester too, which I did. I phoned them all—June at home, Chester at home too. I know I tried Chester at his office, and then at the club, but he'd gone home early that day. Dan I didn't track down until later. He and Arlene weren't home when I called and I left a message on their machine to phone me at Mom's as soon as he got in. He finally called around eight, I think, and he'd been—I can't recall where. Out of town is all I can remember."

Dale said, "Isn't it time to bring the cops back into this? This is what they're paid to do. Why should Don do their job? Let Bill Stankie round up all the Osbornes and drag them into his back room and grill them one by one, and then go out and check out their stories. That should narrow down the list of family suspects fast enough."

I explained that it was of limited use to repeat to the police either Craig's story of the jewel robbery to save the *Herald* or his accusations of homicide against his father because Craig had vowed to deny to the police and the prosecutors that he had told me anything at all. I said, "I could fill Bill Stankie in confidentially, but at this point there isn't much he can do with the information. He certainly can't put the interrogatory thumbscrews to Chester—or June, or Tidy—on the word of a convicted murderer and jewel thief and notorious liar."

Janet, Dale, and Timmy were listening solemnly as I laid out this frustrating addendum to my revelations of the past hour—when we heard a sudden shriek from inside the house.

A cop car was supposedly parked across the street, but my fear was that somehow an attacker had entered the house and gotten to Ruth Osborne. I led the way as we hurtled through the kitchen—Timmy not so fast on crutches—and down the dim hall and into Tom Osborne's study.

But no intruder was present. Ruth Osborne stood alone at her husband's library table. The urn with the label that read "WILLIAM T. "TOM" OSBORNE—1911–1989" was resting on the table. The lid had been removed and lay next to the urn. Mrs. Osborne stood staring with a look of horror into the urn. Her eyes came up to us, and she cried out, "Where is my husband! This urn contains cornmeal! Where is my husband!"

20

At first I thought Mrs. Osborne's mind was faltering again. But when I looked down at the brass container on the table, its contents were indeed fine-grained and pale yellow.

Looking both disgusted and fearful, Janet said, "Mom, how do you know that's cornmeal? It doesn't look like bone fragments, but . . . how can you tell what it is?"

"I tasted it." Mrs. Osborne's big hands were trembling and her face twisted with grief. "It looked like cornmeal, so I tasted it, and please take my word for it, that's what it is. But where are Tom's ashes? Someone has taken Tom's ashes and substituted cornmeal. Why in God's name would anyone do something so cruel? Is this—is it some pathetic joke one of you has pulled on me?"

"Of course not, Mom! We'd never do anything as ridiculous as that. What were you doing getting into Dad's ashes anyway? I know you like having them around, and I can more or less understand that. But why do you want to look at them? I really can't see how that gravelly stuff can ever remind you of Dad."

Looking flustered and annoyed, Mrs. Osborne said, "I decided to scatter the ashes out-of-doors, as your father said he wanted done, and as you and Eric and Dan always said I should do. Well, I was finally going to let you all have your way. I called Slim Finn a while ago and asked him if there was any legal reason I couldn't spread Tom around in my herb garden. Slim said not if it would make me feel better, and not if word didn't get around Edensburg, and not if nobody ever found out he expressed an opinion on the subject. So forget I ever mentioned Slim."

Janet said, "In your herb garden, Mom? Mom, Dad wanted his ashes dropped over the mountains from the air. Isn't spreading him in the backyard a little—shall we say—more *domestic* than what Dad had in mind?"

"It seemed to me a reasonable compromise," Mrs. Osborne said. "In marriage there's always give-and-take."

I asked, "When was the last time, Mrs. Osborne, that you looked inside the urn and saw what appeared to be your husband's actual remains?"

She grimaced and stared into space. Remembering was a struggle for her, and she seemed to be laboring almost physically. "Quite a while ago," she said after a moment. "A year or two, I suppose. It's been a while since I actually lifted the lid and looked in. It's true that all that stony stuff just looks like stony stuff, and it doesn't help much in summoning up Tom's memory and spirit."

"Who has access to this study besides yourself, Mrs. Osborne? Who's gone in here in the past two years? From the look of the place, I'd guess the traffic hasn't been heavy."

"No, no, hardly anybody comes into this musty old room. Just myself, and Elsie to clean. The children, I suppose, from time to time, to look at their father's books and papers. Janet, you've been in, of course—but you didn't get into the urn, did you?"

"Mother, of course not!"

"Dan comes in once in a while—and June once in a blue moon. June's husband, Dick, perhaps. Chester? I don't believe so. Chester generally comes in the back door, shakes his fist at me in the kitchen, and leaves by the same route." Then she seemed to go blank.

Timmy said, "What about workmen or other outsiders, Mrs. Osborne? Have you had any electrical or telephone or other work done in this room in the last few years?"

Both the old black Bakelite telephone and the wall sconces, as well as the metal gooseneck desk lamp, looked as if they dated to the first Roosevelt administration, and Mrs. Osborne said, "Does this room look as if anyone has replaced a single item in it in the last half century? We should have done some modernizing—I always approve of technological progress if it frees people up to get on with what's truly important—but I can't recall anybody coming in here to fix or replace anything in years and years. No, no workmen stole Tom's ashes, I don't

144

think, and filled the urn up with cornmeal. It must have been someone in the family, is all I can think. Tidy has been in the house from time to time—and Tacker before he flew the coop. But why would either of them do such a thing?"

Dale said, "What about Eric?"

Mrs. Osborne's face drooped, and she said, "Well, naturally Eric came in here often. He borrowed books—which he always was careful to return—and he read Tom's files and papers. He liked being around Tom's things, just as I do. Eric loved his father and enjoyed being around him so terribly much, and after Tom was gone Eric liked coming in here and regaining a sense of the man. But why would Eric steal Tom's ashes without telling me, and what in heaven's name would he ever do with them?"

Janet gave Dale a quick glance, and Timmy gave me one. Janet said, "Mom, did Eric know that you sometimes actually looked inside the urn at Dad's ashes?"

"Of course not. There was no need for him to know. Not that he would have found it peculiar, I'm sure. Lord knows what June would have said, or Chester—it was just too morbid, those two would surely insist. Eric, on the other hand, would have understood—as I'm sure you do, Janet. And Dale, of course. But, still, there was no need, really, to tell him I ever looked inside the urn, so I didn't."

"Mom," Janet said, "Eric was the one of us who was most upset when you didn't follow Dad's wishes and scatter his ashes over the mountains. Don't you remember what a pain in the neck Eric was over that?"

"Yes, he was upset with me."

"He nagged at you for months."

"Years."

"He saw it as some kind of betrayal of trust."

"Yes, Eric made a moral issue out of it. He thought gravel tossed to the winds was more important than my mental comfort. We disagreed about that."

"So maybe Eric took the ashes," Janet said, "and scattered them over the mountains himself. He figured—you know—what you didn't know wouldn't hurt you."

Mrs. Osborne's face tightened. She said, "What a dishonest thing to do. It doesn't sound at all like Eric."

"I suppose his rationale would have been that since you went against

Dad's wishes in this one matter, he could go against yours."

Looking hurt, she said, "But I'm not dead."

Janet sighed deeply. "You're right, Mom. If Eric did take the ashes, he should not have done it without at least admitting it to you afterward so you wouldn't open the urn one day and find this . . . stuff. That was wrong."

"Well," Mrs. Osborne said, "I suppose what's done is done. If indeed that's what happened. Is there some way we can verify that it was Eric who took the ashes? I do need to know that, if only for my own peace of mind. Eric I can forgive, of course, but I do need to know for certain exactly what has become of my husband's remains."

"Mrs. Osborne, I think I can do some detective work on the ashes," I said. "In fact, the mystery of the missing ashes may be directly related to another puzzling disappearance I was about to begin working on." Janet looked at me expressionlessly and nodded. She knew. Dale and Timmy looked my way too, and lightbulbs went on over their heads.

"I'll eagerly await the results of your investigation, Mr. Strachey. For now, I guess I won't be spreading my husband's ashes in my herb garden. But I am going to put out some sweet corn and tomatoes on the table in a little while. I've got some barbecued beef in the freezer I can zap and heat up. And how would you all feel about some fresh corn bread to go with it?"

Janet said, "Oh, you don't need to bother with the corn bread, Mom. I can pick up a couple of sourdough baguettes." The relief in the room was palpable.

21

We wondered why Mr. Osborne's remains glittered the way they did," Skeeter said. "It was just after sunrise on a Sunday morning during the first week in April. The pilot circled around after Eric emptied the urn out the side window of the plane, and we all said, hey, look how Mr. Osborne's ashes are glimmering and glittering in the sunlight. Isn't that beautiful!"

Timmy and I were seated next to Skeeter's bed in his room at Albany Med. Janet and Dale had remained behind with Mrs. Osborne with two Edensburg police officers watching over them, one in the front of the house, one in the rear.

Skeeter had been off the prednisone for ninety-six hours, and his sanity was pretty much back. He was also recovering well, he told us, from the pneumocystis pneumonia, and he expected to be out of the hospital in a day or two. Some Edensburg friends of his and Eric's had been looking after him and planned on taking him into their home until he was back on his feet. Skeeter had lost weight, but his strength was returning and he hoped to be back on the job with the park service in a few weeks. When we described the hotel robbery to him and told him of the likelihood that Dan had hidden the stolen jewels in the urn with Tom Osborne's ashes, Skeeter was stunned at first. Then he remarked on how the ashes glinted in the sunlight as they drifted down. He also added, "God, I wonder if Eric knew."

I looked at Timmy, who was seated beside Skeeter holding his big hairy hand. Timmy looked at me, and we both looked back at Skeeter.

I said, "How might Eric have known the jewels were in the ashes?"

"I don't know, and I think he would have told me if he'd known there was anything valuable in there. We always told each other really important stuff. But maybe Eric wanted to protect me from guilty knowledge that could get me in trouble with the park service. That's something old Eric might have done for me," Skeeter said bleakly, the grief showing in his face all over again.

"You two were really a great pair," Timmy said. "I'm so, so sorry you lost Eric, Skeeter."

"Eric was the great love of my life," Skeeter said, his voice quavering. "Until I met Eric, I never knew how strong and real love could be between two men. If I'd never met Eric, I might have gone my entire life without loving and being loved by another man."

Timmy colored a little, squeezed Skeeter's hand, and said, "Oh."

"Before Eric there was all that great sex, of course," Skeeter said. "And I can't say I didn't love it. Most of it, anyway. But by the time I met Eric I wanted more than that. Jeez, I was so lucky I found him."

Releasing Skeeter's hand, Timmy said, "Where did you two meet, anyway?"

Skeeter chuckled. "Under a bush in Washington Park in Albany."

"Very romantic."

"It really was," Skeeter said, grinning through his thick beard. "Winter wasn't so great, but those summer nights were pretty wonderful sometimes."

"Timothy and I met under similar circumstances," I said, and Timmy smiled weakly.

"Was Don your first great love?" Skeeter asked.

Timmy stared at him and his lower lip twitched.

I said, "Not the first for either of us, Skeeter, but the deepest and longest."

Timmy said, "True, true."

While Timmy sat pensively, I told Skeeter I thought it was likely that Eric's murder was in some way connected with the lost jewels, since their purpose had been to generate cash that would save the *Herald* for the Osbornes.

"Damn, yes, that must be it!" Skeeter said. "But who besides Dan and Craig would have known that Eric knew about the jewels—if he did? Or do you think"—his dark eyes hardened—"do you think Dan could have had something to do with Eric's murder?"

148

I said I didn't know, that Dan was missing and I was unable to question him.

"Dan is moody and weird," Skeeter said, "but I really can't imagine him hurting anybody physically. Especially Eric. They were different, but in a way they understood and appreciated each other amazingly well. And I certainly can't see Dan trying to get Janet run over by a Jet Ski. Anyway, if somebody tried to run Dan and Arlene off a cliff, then somebody's after them too. Unless he faked all that. Which, according to Eric, is the type of thing Dan used to do in his anti–Vietnam War days."

I told Skeeter that Arlene at least seemed to be a reliable witness to the road incident. Then I laid out Craig's theory that Chester had assumed Eric was in on the jewel-theft plot and killed Eric when he refused to acknowledge his complicity and turn over the proceeds from the heist to the conservative side of the Osborne family.

Skeeter's face tightened and he shifted angrily in the bed. "Chester! That jerk. Maybe it *was* him."

"Craig thinks so," I said, "but this is the speculation of a son who has apparently despised his father since childhood and isn't as objective as he could be."

"But Chester was always violent. You must have heard the stories."

I reminded Skeeter that Chester's outbursts had always been spontaneous, not premeditated, and I asked, "Would Chester have been out on a hiking trail where he might have run into Eric? Or would he actually have gone hiking with Eric?"

Skeeter shook his head morosely. "As far as I know, Chester hasn't been out on a hiking trail in years. In family pictures you can see him in the woods as a kid, but that was just because he had to. Chester was an Osborne, so he went into the wilderness. But as soon as he could choose, he headed for the country club."

Timmy said, "Skeeter, is there some chance that Eric was in on the jewel-theft plot? Not that he would want anybody to get killed. But maybe Craig had promised him and Dan nobody would get hurt and the robbery was a foolproof way to keep the *Herald* out of the hands of the bad chain, and Eric was naive enough to believe him."

"Out of the hands of what?" Skeeter looked deeply bewildered.

Timmy forced a little smile and said, "There are two newspaper chains competing for the *Herald*. One's a good chain, and one's a bad chain. One's a daisy chain—that's a metaphor for the more socially enlightened, pro-environmentalist chain—and one's a chain of fools, so-called. The chain of fools is purely profit-oriented and environmentally and otherwise socially indifferent. It was you, Skeeter, as a matter of fact, who first explained this situation to Don and me and pointed out the likelihood that one of the Osborne factions competing over the future of the *Herald* had concocted a murder plot that resulted in Eric's death and presented great danger to Janet prior to next month's *Herald* board meeting."

Timmy fingered the two crutches—his own—leaning against Skeeter's bed. I wondered if he might pick one of them up and swat Skeeter with it, but he didn't. He said, "You were heavily medicated when you expressed your concerns to Don and me Tuesday night, Skeeter. So I guess all this has slipped your mind."

"You're right, it has," Skeeter said, looking embarrassed. "I remember that you and Don were here on Tuesday, or whatever day it was. And even though I was kind of out of it, I also remember from when you and Janet stopped in on Wednesday, I guess it was, Timmy, that you told me you and Don have been helping out around the house. And also, Don, that you've been playing detective. Hey, good for you. Thanks a lot from all of us. And Timmy, I want to tell you it's really great to be in touch with you again. Since my folks moved to Arizona, I'm hardly in touch with anybody back in Poughkeepsie. But you were always one of my favorite high-school classmates. It's really nice to see you."

Timmy smiled just perceptibly. He said, "It's really nice to see you too, Skeeter."

Skeeter had given us the name of the air service Eric had used for scattering his father's ashes over the mountains, and as we headed back up to Edensburg, and to the airport there, Timmy was silent for the first ten miles.

Finally, I said, "I think he was just being considerate of me—of both of us. Or maybe he thinks you never told me that you two were once a red-hot item."

After a moment, Timmy said, "That's pretty far-fetched."

"Why? Some people are just very discreet about their pasts."

He said nothing for a mile or so. Then: "Could I have imagined the whole thing? Am I delusionary? Or was I delusionary in high school? Maybe my whole two-year sexfest with Skeeter took place entirely inside my own head. It was just tortured, conflicted, wishful thinking."

"Not according to what Skeeter was saying Tuesday night when he OD'd on prednisone," I said. "The drug seemed to be working as a truth serum on Skeeter, and the affair was certainly real enough to him then."

"Maybe the prednisone worked as a truth serum, or maybe it made him temporarily insane too, and he was imagining it all."

"Timothy, I can see how you're feeling disoriented and confused at this point, but keep in mind that it's Skeeter who's more likely to be delusionary. His brain was given a ferocious whack by a heavy-duty steroid drug. And I hate to say it, but there's also the possibility of the onset of HIV dementia. I doubt very much that it's you who is mixed up about the past."

Timmy shook his head fiercely, as if to try to loosen a mental ice jam. He moaned, "I don't know!" and then slumped in his seat.

After we'd sped up the Northway another mile, I said, "So where was Skeeter's birthmark?"

Timmy shifted, sat up a little, gazed over at me. "How did you know about that?"

"Skeeter mentioned it Tuesday night while you were out of the hospital room. He mentioned that you were once mighty pleased with that birthmark of his, but he didn't tell me where it was. Where was it?"

Timmy grinned. "I guess I'm not crazy."

"Of course not. Did you really think you were?"

"No. But I am confused, and it helps that you've come up with actual incontrovertible evidence that I'm not hallucinating. It all did happen, and it's Skeeter who's losing his mind. Poor Skeeter."

"So where is it?"

"The birthmark?"

"The birthmark."

"It's on the back of his dick. When it's limp, the birthmark has no particular discernible shape. But when Skeeter's penis is erect, the birthmark is shaped exactly like the state of North Carolina. If it was standing on end, of course."

"I guess you would tend to make a mental note of something like that. Is Skeeter originally from the South?"

151

"No, he was born in Poughkeepsie and grew up about a mile from our house."

"I'll bet the McCaslins were originally from Dixie. How else to explain this remarkable phenomenon? I think Skeeter should send an inscribed photo of his erection to Jesse Helms."

After a moment, Timmy said, "So if I *didn't* ruin the first half of Skeeter's adulthood—or if I did but he's actually forgotten all about it, I guess I didn't really have to drag you—drag both of us—into this whole Osborne family morass of murder and intrigue. I didn't have to get you involved, I didn't have to get my foot broken, and I didn't have to get into a situation where I'm maligned and abused by Dale Kotlowicz every time I'm in the room with that merciless, unrelenting, sarcastic harpie."

"Much of what you say is true, Timothy, although I'm confident your opinion of Dale will go up once the air has been cleared on your alleged transgression. Surely it's all a simple misunderstanding. So, are you removing me from the Osborne case? Am I fired? Shall we drive past Edensburg and up to Montreal for a relaxed weekend of jazz and French food and afternoon strolls along the waterfront?"

"Of course not. Jeez. Janet is depending on us now. And so is Mrs. Osborne. And even—other people."

"Dale."

"Yes, Dale too. Dale, Dale, Dale, Dale."

He shifted in his seat again, careful not to get conked on the head by his crutches.

I'd phoned Eden County Air Service from Albany. The pilot who had taken Eric and Skeeter up the previous April to scatter Tom Osborne's ashes over the Adirondacks was away for the day, ferrying a canoe-company executive to Rochester and back. He was expected in around 11:30 P.M., so Timmy and I had time for a sandwich at a diner near the Edensburg airport before we met the charter pilot on his late-evening arrival.

The pilot, a placid, alert-looking man in his late twenties, remembered Eric and Skeeter well—he'd known the Osbornes by reputation for years—and when I told him I was working for Janet, he told me how much he respected and admired her and the *Herald*. Then he went on to tell me everything he knew about the April excursion.

The pilot did recall the "glitter" of the ashes as they drifted down toward the forest just after sunrise on April 4th. He said he had spread ashes on three previous occasions for other mourners and had never seen ashes sparkle before. He said both Skeeter and Eric seemed as surprised as he was by the glittering display.

The pilot also told us, in answer to a question of mine, that Dan Osborne had—a month or so after the dispersal of the ashes—tracked the pilot down, questioned him about the scattering of the ashes, and paid him to fly Dan over the precise spot where the ashes had been tossed from the plane.

The pilot had done so and had, at Dan's request, marked the area on a topographical map where the ashes would likely have landed in the forest. Because of the relatively low flying altitude of about 1,500 feet, as well as the calm air that day, the probable landing area for the ashes could be narrowed down to about three square miles. Dan had told the pilot he was interested in the ashes' location "for sentimental reasons," which the pilot had had no reason to disbelieve. The pilot helpfully provided me with a map showing the area he had directed Dan to, about twelve miles west of Edensburg.

22

It was close to one A.M. when Timmy and I returned to Maple Street, and while the rest of the neighborhood was dark, the Osborne house was ablaze with light. A police patrol car was parked in front of the house, with two officers visible in the front seat, their foam coffee cups on the dashboard.

Inside the house, I was relieved to find that Mrs. Osborne was safe and had gone to bed, and that Janet and Dale were safe and still up; I wanted to recruit them for an expedition early the next morning to visit the three square miles of mountainside west of Edensburg where I was certain we would find Dan Osborne combing the woods for the $16 million worth of jewels, and where we could use our knowledge of Dan's aiding and abetting a felony to extract from him answers to questions about the sale of the *Herald,* Eric's murder, and Dan's hypersensitive stomach.

Janet and Dale, however, were not alone on the back porch. "Don, Timmy, I want you to meet Lee Ann Stasiowski," Janet said, and introduced us to the woman who had stuck her head in Janet's office door with a message from Dale the day before. Lee Ann was a tiny, hazel-eyed middle-aged woman with a gray-blond pixie cut, a reporter's notebook in one hand and a bottle of Sam Adams in the other. She was the *Herald*'s reporter, Janet told us, who had once covered police and the courts and now wrote about business. Lee Ann had been reporting in recent months—in a circumspect way—on the *Herald*'s own financial difficulties and impending sale to a chain.

"And now," Janet said, "it's time for Lee Ann to prepare a story on the latest developments in the situation—that is, attempts on the lives of pro-Griscomb family members and a developing connection between the sale of the paper and Eric's murder."

Lee Ann said, "I'm amazed to hear about all this wild stuff. Well, I'm amazed and I'm not so amazed."

This exercise in aggressive good journalism struck me as premature and maybe reckless. I said, "I don't know. Is this for Sunday's paper or Monday's?"

"It's for later," Janet said. "It'll run sometime next week, or the week after—whenever Lee Ann's got the entire story, including who's been arrested for murder and/or attempted murder."

"What I'm gathering right now," Lee Ann said, "is background, most of which I'm getting from Janet and Dale. I'm also—on Janet's excellent suggestion—using your involvement in the case, Don, as an excuse to grill Osborne family members on Eric's murder. I'm telling any Osborne I talk to that since a private detective is investigating them, I'm reporting on his activities as much as I am any possible family connection to Eric's death. That way they can vent about you—and, believe me, they do, they do—and at the same time I can ask them, almost in passing, where they were on the morning Eric was murdered, and do they have an alibi, should they need one."

Dale said, "Cagey, huh?"

"Very clever," Timmy said. "Good for you, Janet."

"It was Dale's idea," Janet said. "Chester and June are both fuming, naturally. And Stu Torkildson called me a couple of hours ago and said he would never dream of interfering in the editorial side of the paper, and if he did, at least three Osbornes would be spinning in their graves. But wasn't it likely, Stu suggested in his oleaginous, vaguely threatening way, that Lee Ann's investigation at this point might spook Info-Com or Griscomb or any other potential buyer, and the family might get left in the lurch altogether?"

"Torkildson took that line with me too," I said. "What did you tell him?"

"That the news is the news," Janet said, "and the *Herald* reports the news. Stu didn't see it that way, but it's not my impression that when Lee Ann's story is set, Stu will hurl himself bodily into the presses to sabotage the run. That's not the way he operates."

"How does he operate?" I said.

"Legally. He's greedy and he's cunning, but Stu comes from a Glens

Falls family that's produced judges and brain surgeons and even some honest politicians, and his name and reputation mean as much to him as money does. So I don't think he'll interfere. But Stu will bear watching, of course," Janet said, and we all agreed solemnly with that.

I asked Lee Ann which Osbornes she had interviewed and what she had learned.

"I just got started around five this afternoon," she said, "so I've only seen three so far. June and Dick Puderbaugh had plenty of opinions— about the *Herald*'s editorial page, about the paper's future ownership, and about you, Don—but nothing that sounded to me especially useful in the murder investigation. They both had alibis that could easily be checked out. Dick spent the morning, he said, in his office with his secretary and bookkeeper, as he does every weekday morning. And June was at the art museum with Parson and Evangeline Bates helping hang the canoes-at-sunrise show.

"I had trouble getting Chester to talk to me at all. I called his home, and he answered, and I described to him as best I could the story I was working on. But he kept interrupting and telling me how irresponsible it would be for me to be quoting slanderous statements from family members and from people he called 'outsiders.' My conversation with Chester was also confusing and hard to sort out because all the time Chester was talking, I could hear Pauline yelling at him and carrying on something awful in the background."

"What was she yelling?" I asked. "Could you make it out?"

"Not much of it," Lee Ann said. "Sometimes she just seemed to be screaming uncontrollably. But I could decipher a word or sentence now and then. I caught, 'She's your fucking mother!' and something about 'fucking muddy feet!' And once I'm sure she yelled, 'I ought to get another gun and blow your fucking brains out!' My impression was, Pauline had had a few drinks."

I said, "Chester must have taken the gun she waved at me away from her. Which was a good idea. So you were only able to interview Chester on the phone?"

Lee Ann chugged from her beer bottle and said, "No, he actually agreed to meet me. He said his nephew was visiting and the television was on loud at his place—as if he lived in a studio apartment—so he said he'd meet me at nine at the *Herald*, which he did. He sounded real rattled, and I kept remembering all those stories about Chester's violent temper, which I've never seen. But he showed up on time, and we talked in the conference room after he shut the door with a DO NOT DISTURB sign he wrote and taped on the outside."

"Who would the nephew be?" I asked Janet. She looked back at me blankly.

"My impression was that was just a line," Lee Ann said. "The 'noisy television' was Pauline hollering, and Chester wanted to get the hell out of there. And I think also that he wanted to get me alone, in the flesh, so he could make a lot of veiled and unveiled threats that would make me back off the story."

"Physical threats?" Timmy asked.

"No, just legal. But Chester can get himself worked up into a state. Everybody in town knows that. I was glad there were people right outside the door in the newsroom. Anyway, he gave me his whole Info-Com pitch—which we all know by heart by now—and next to nothing on the attacks on Janet and Dan, which he claims are either imagined or contrived. And as for Eric's murder, the very idea of family involvement is slanderous if spoken, Chester warned me, and libelous if the *Herald* prints it.

"The one possibly useful piece of information I got from Chester is this: He may not have an alibi for the time of the murder. He went into a three-alarm swivet when I asked him where he was on the morning of May fifteenth, and when I seemed to be calmly noting his hotheaded unresponsiveness, he made an effort to settle down, and he said, well, he was in his office. I asked him if I—or the police—could verify that with witnesses and appointment records, and then he totally lost it. He jumped up, and he was shaking and towering over me and yelling that I could just goddamn well accept his word for where he was if I valued my job. When I eased out of my chair and opened the door to the newsroom, Chester shoved his way past me and stormed out of the place. I really thought the next thing would be the sound of his Lexus doing a couple of donuts in the parking lot before he peeled out. But I guess that's not Chester's style. He just drove away normally."

I said, "All this is extremely helpful, Lee Ann. Who do you plan on interviewing next?"

"Tidy in the morning, if he'll talk to me, and—for the record—Dale and Skeeter McCaslin. I don't plan to be bound by conventional notions of family."

"Thank you, Lee Ann," Dale said. "I'll cooperate fully with your investigation."

"After that," Lee Ann said, "I'll talk to nonfamily peripheral people like Stu Torkildson and Parson Bates. I might also drive out to Attica and visit Craig Osborne. Janet filled me in on the jewel-robbery angle. It all sounds like a pretty wacky way to try to save the *Herald*. But the fourth generation of Osbornes produced some extremely wacky people, so—hey, why not?"

Janet asked me if Skeeter had been able to verify that in April Eric had spirited away his father's remains from the urn on Ruth Osborne's mantel, and I said Skeeter had. I told Janet, Dale, and Lee Ann that Skeeter, Eric, and the charter pilot had all remarked at the time on how glittery the falling ashes were, and I explained how Dan had later sought out the pilot wanting to learn where the ashes had settled to earth.

"So that must be where Dan is now!" Janet said. "Do you have the directions?"

I said I did and held up my map. "My guess is, he's out there sifting one more time through several square miles of wilderness that I'll bet he's combed a hundred times since April. He'd like to find the diamonds and make a last-ditch attempt to save the *Herald* for the Osbornes. And, I'm sure, Dan wants desperately to be able to tell Craig he recovered the jewels. He knows Craig is mad as hell and is starting to talk to people, foremost among them me."

"God," Janet said, "Dan is such a nitwit!"

"The robbery was bad enough," Dale said. "But you'd think he'd have had enough sense to stash the loot in a safe-deposit box."

We all speculated for some minutes on the practical, Freudian, and other reasons Dan might have had for mixing the stolen gems with his father's ashes in an urn on his mother's mantel.

We were about to make a plan for heading out to find Dan in the morning when headlights suddenly arched across the backyard and a car screeched to a halt in the driveway. The cop car must have pulled in directly behind the visitor, for three car doors slammed and then there were raised voices, one female.

While Timmy was reaching for his crutches, the rest of us moved fast. Dale barricaded herself at the foot of the stairs leading to the second floor, where Mrs. Osborne was sleeping, and Janet, Lee Ann, and

I trotted out into the muggy night and found the two Edensburg cops attempting to subdue Pauline Osborne. Chester's wife was unarmed, as far as we could see, but she was unsteady on her feet and flailing at the two cops physically and verbally.

"What the hell are you gorillas bothering me for, when it's my husband who's a criminal! You want to arrest a criminal, arrest Chester Osborne—Chester Osborne, the big murderer! Why don't you go up there and arrest him right now? I'll testify! I'll go to court! I'll swear on a stack of Bibles that the day Chester's brother Eric was murdered, Chester came home covered with leaves and mud!"

The two cops, both young, baby-faced, and portly, were listening to this recitation with obvious interest while at the same time making occasional perfunctory grabs for the tanned and braceleted arms Pauline was waving around. In peach-colored slacks and a white halter top, Pauline was elegantly put together and nicely limber. But her mascara and green eye shadow had run down over cheeks that were flushed from alcohol and excitement, and her face looked disconcertingly like a summer storm system moving across the radar screen on the Weather Channel.

"Pauline, why don't you come in for some coffee?" Janet said. Then, maybe realizing that this casual invitation sounded too inane for the occasion, she added, "Or you could come in and suck down another half bottle of whatever's got you skunked, and then sleep it off under the kitchen table. Either way, we should talk."

The cops had been barking out things like "Hey, missus! Hey—hey, missus!" and they seemed to know that they should be taking matters in hand—there were murder accusations and drunk driving at a minimum here—but they also had figured out that this raving woman was Mrs. Chester Osborne, and this fact also must have carried weight with them.

I said, "I think you officers can see that Mrs. Osborne would do well to get off the highway, and we'd be happy to keep her car keys overnight and make sure she's safe—"

"No! No!" Pauline snarled. "I will *not* get off the highway—I will not rest until somebody arrests Chester Osborne for murder! That man is a killer, and I'll bet your bottom dollar Tacker Puderbaugh was in on it too! They're in cahoots—why else would Tacker be up at our house? He's supposed to be out of the country on his surfboard. Chester was

160

covered with mud the day Eric got killed, and Tacker was in on it! Hey, I'm for bringin' in the bucks. But I draw the line at murdering nice people like Eric. Chester and Tacker Puderbaugh have to be arrested right now! I demand it! As a taxpayer, I demand that you arrest my husband, who's that goddamn big murderer Chester Osborne!"

It was at this point that the other Osborne shiny Lexus, the black one, cruised noiselessly into the driveway, and Chester got out and walked over to us. His posture wasn't up to standard, the sweat on his big Osborne face glistened, and in shirtsleeves and no tie he looked vulnerable and a little desperate.

Chester said to all of us, "I can just imagine what kind of b.s. my wife has been spreading down here, and I'm here to tell you, it's goddamn not true. Pauline is inebriated, I'm goddamn sorry to say, and she's confused in the head. My attorney, Morton Bond, is on his way over here now. I just got off the phone with him. And if you officers will get somebody over here from the DA's office"—Chester glared at his wife bitterly now—"I'm prepared to make a statement."

"A statement about what?" Janet said, her face darkening. "A statement about Eric's murder?"

"Hell, no," Chester said, "not about Eric's murder, goddamn it! Do you really think I'd kill my own brother, Janet, even if he *was* some fruitcake eco-Nazi! Jesus Christ, Janet! No, I'll make a statement about Tacker Puderbaugh, my idiotic nephew, who was supposed to—to just do a couple of mischievous things to scare you and Dan into possibly changing your vote on the sale of the paper. But I'm goddamn sorry to say that Tacker Puderbaugh is out of control. He went way too far tonight, and he tried to involve me in what he did tonight, and I'm here to tell you I did not—did *not*—give Tacker an okay on that."

"What did Tacker do?" Janet said.

Chester shook his head and said grimly, "He burned your house down, Janet. It was totally uncalled for."

That's when the phone began to ring inside the house. The distraction was brief, but it was just long enough for us to miss grabbing Pauline before she walked over to Chester and got him by the neck and began to scream and squeeze.

23

In fact, two phone calls came at the Osborne house, one after the other. The first was from the Eden County Sheriff's office notifying Janet that her house at Stilton Lake had been badly damaged by fire, but not destroyed, a few hours earlier. The deputy wanted to verify that no one had been inside the house at the time. Janet said no one had, and she and Dale soon left for the lake. I offered to accompany them, but they said no, they'd call some friends who lived nearby. They did, and their friends said they would call other friends—a circle of friends made up mainly of members of the Hot Flashes Softball League—and they would all meet Janet and Dale at the fire scene.

Janet was shaky and angry but in control, and she urged that I remain behind to help look after her mother and to stay on top of the investigation, which Janet said had taken a turn that was "sickening but not all that surprising."

Dale, thoughtful and much subdued, said there were still too many unanswered questions, and we all agreed with that. Timmy, balanced on his crutches, muttered about a good chain and a bad chain, a daisy chain and a chain of fools, and Lee Ann took notes.

Just after Janet and Dale drove off, the phone rang again. This one was a call for me from the investigative agency in Los Angeles I had asked to track down Tacker Puderbaugh. I was informed that Tacker had departed Papeete for the United States on July 17, two weeks before the first Jet Ski attack on Janet but more than two months after Eric's murder. If Tacker had not left Tahiti, he might have had his visa revoked and been ordered to leave the French colony, my informant said. Tacker had been arrested twice on minor drug charges and once for shoplifting beer.

Out in the driveway, Pauline had been handcuffed and locked in the back of the cruiser, from which her angry screams issued forth intermittently. It was after two A.M., and lights had come on in some of the neighboring houses. Two teenage boys and a middle-aged woman stood watching the scene from the front porch of a house across Maple Street. Ruth Osborne apparently was sleeping soundly. We could hear the hum of her air conditioner above us.

I phoned Bill Stankie at home and woke him up. He said he was glad I'd called with my five-minute update on the investigation, but, he said, it was not yet time for him to involve himself in the Osborne drama if the only evidence available so far concerned arson and attempted murder. It was Eric's homicide he wanted to pin on Chester, if he could, and Stankie asked if I thought Chester had done it. I said, no, I didn't, but I wasn't sure.

After a thoughtful pause, Stankie said, "You're doing excellent work, Don. Keep at it, and stay in touch. I'm going back to sleep." Then he hung up.

Another town police department patrol car soon arrived, its flashers flashing as it cruised down otherwise deserted Maple Street. Perhaps the spectacular light show was to warn worms that were thinking of crossing the road. A uniformed police sergeant got out and identified himself as a detective. A young woman carrying a tape recorder and a thermos accompanied the detective, and he introduced her as the assistant DA who was to depose Chester. Then Chester's lawyer arrived, a jowly, bleary-eyed man with a briefcase. He was dressed for court, silk tie and all, and looked almost ashamed of the motley assemblage he found before him. I had on jeans, sandals, and a faded yellow T-shirt, and Timmy was wearing a tank top, running shorts, and several pounds of fiberglass.

Chester sat in his car and conferred with his lawyer for five minutes. Then we all trooped into the house, where Chester, the lawyer, the police sergeant, and the assistant DA went into the study with the urn full of cornmeal resting on the mantel. They shut the door. I'd asked if I could sit in, but Chester's lawyer said no. Timmy, Lee Ann, and I considered ways of eavesdropping, but then thought better of it.

Just after 3:15, the four came out. Timmy was sound asleep on a chaise on the back porch, but Lee Ann and I were upright, if not fully alert. Lee Ann asked the prosecutor if charges would be brought against Chester. The young woman said she would have to discuss that with her boss and otherwise she could not comment.

Chester's lawyer said, "Mr. Osborne made some remarks to his nephew that were misinterpreted, and the young man seems to have run amok. Mr. Osborne denies that he is in any way responsible for any illegal acts Tacker Puderbaugh may have committed. Mr. Osborne is cooperating fully with law enforcement, and the police are now looking for young Tacker. We expect that an arrest warrant will be issued in the morning—which is fast approaching."

I said, "Do you expect Tacker to corroborate your client's description of events?"

The lawyer looked at me carefully and said, "That kid has always been an asshole, and I'm sure he'll be looking for a way out of the deep pile of shit he's in now. But nobody in his right mind is going to accept some dopehead beach bum's word over Chester Osborne's."

"Tacker's mother might," I said. The lawyer looked bleak. The thought of tangling with June could not have made him look forward to the dawn. Chester looked somber too, and his face didn't brighten when I added, "Pauline Osborne has some additional pertinent information." I asked the DA, "Are you going to be talking to her?"

"Sure," the young woman said. "Although I understand Mr. Osborne has initiated commitment proceedings against his wife on the grounds that she is a danger to herself and to others. Mr. Osborne just informed me that a hearing is likely on Monday."

"Yes," Osborne's lawyer said, "it's unlikely that this tragically disturbed lady will have anything to say that could be used in anybody's investigation. You've visited with her, I understand. You can see that she's well around the bend."

Timmy, Lee Ann, and I stared at Chester, who stood looking at us with no expression at all.

I said, "Chester, what are you planning on doing? Having all the Osborne women who won't let you have your way locked up?"

He said, "I would if I could." But then his lawyer signaled for Chester to say no more, and they left.

165

24

Dan and Arlene had leased a Range Rover to replace the one damaged when they'd been run off the road. I found the vehicle parked at the edge of an old logging trail on the mountainside where the ashes and diamonds had rained down in April. Their tent had been set up nearby, and their cooking fire appeared freshly doused when I discovered the campsite just after seven Saturday morning. I knew the tent was theirs because several items of clothing hanging on a branch looked like Arlene's, and the tent smelled of pot.

Neither Dan nor Arlene was present at the camp, and I tramped around in the nearby woods for the next hour without locating them—or finding millions of dollars' worth of jewels in the underbrush—before I wised up and hiked back to the campsite to await Dan and Arlene's inevitable return.

When I heard them approaching just after ten, I was inside the tent sitting on a campstool, trying to read Dan's copy of *The Autumn of the Patriarch*. It was in the original Spanish, but I grasped a word here and there: *sí, no, nada, muerto,* etc.

"Yo, Dan. Hey there, Arlene," I yelled, and Arlene shrieked. "Hey, it's just me—Strachey."

The tent flap was flung aside, and Dan stood there glaring and breathing hard. As Arlene came up behind him and leaned down to get a glimpse of the intruder, Dan snorted at me, "What the fuck are you doing here!"

"Reading your book. I hope you don't mind. I saved your page. And I want you to know, I'm impressed. I couldn't even get through this one in English, and I'm a big García Márquez fan."

167

"Get out of my tent, goddamn it!"

I carefully replaced the novel where I'd found it on the ground cloth next to the double sleeping bag. Dan backed away as I came out into the dappled sunlight. The forest aroma was enchanting after the musty tent smell, but Dan's demeanor—I wondered if he might be going to heave again—meant this would be no time for enchantment.

"Why, Don," Arlene drawled, giving me a forced look of hippie insouciance, "how did you know where to look for us? We were just up here in the woods chilling out for a couple days, and you knew right where to look. That is so weird!"

"I got the map from the charter pilot," I said, and Arlene screamed again. Dan began to retch and staggered off behind some brush.

"Be careful not to puke on the diamonds!" I yelled, and then he really let loose.

Arlene started to follow Dan, but then thought better of it.

I said, "Did he throw up in Cuba too?"

"Some from the turista," she said. "But mostly we just got diarrhea."

"Ahh."

When Dan quieted down, Arlene went to him with a bottle of water. I waited while he attended to his oral hygiene. They both came back a minute later, Dan wan and shaky, bits of his breakfast in his beard.

"I think we need to air some things out," I said.

"I'll get you a clean T-shirt," Arlene told Dan, but he looked at me and he knew what needed airing.

After he changed his shirt, Dan lowered himself to the pine-needled forest floor and leaned against a tree. Arlene and I sat on the two camp stools.

"I talked to Craig," I said. "I talked to the charter pilot. I drew conclusions. I knew to talk to the pilot because your mother discovered that your father's ashes were missing from the urn. If Eric had replaced the ashes with something more human-remains-like than cornmeal, your mother might never have noticed the loss. And none of us would have figured out what happened to the jewels."

Exhaustedly, Dan said, "I put the cornmeal in the urn. Eric had just left it empty. I don't know what the fuck I was thinking."

"God, I don't know either," Arlene said. "You put cornmeal in your father's urn? That gives me the creeps."

"You didn't know about the jewels?" I asked Arlene.

His strength coming back now, Dan snapped, "Arlene didn't know anything until yesterday! So don't go goddamn dragging her into anything. I didn't tell her about the robbery until we got out here, and by then you must have heard about it from Craig, so Arlene was really the last to know and she can't be legally implicated in any way. So just goddamn leave Arlene out of it."

"Sometimes it pisses me off that with Dan I'm always the last one to know anything," Arlene said. "But this time I guess I lucked out. Although, when you come right down to it, Dan didn't really do anything so terrible, and I sure hope the cops aren't going to hassle him. I mean, he didn't even know about the heist until the jewels came in the mail from Craig. By then, I mean, what difference did it make, since those oil sheiks have got diamonds up the wazoo anyway? Dan just thought, hey, he may as well put the jewels to good use and save the *Herald,* and also Craig could get even with his big asshole dad, Chester. So I certainly hope the cops aren't going to make some big fucking deal out of what Dan did."

I looked at Dan, and he glanced at me, and he knew I knew he'd been in on it from the beginning. I said, "It's over, Dan. It's all coming out now. There's no way it can't."

Dan looked away into the woods. Maybe he still thought he'd spot a diamond.

Arlene said, "What's he mean by that, Dan?" He wouldn't look at her or me. She said, "What else is there to come out? What's Don talking about?"

There was a silence, and then Dan said, "Arlene, I need to talk to Strachey privately. I know you're going to be pissed off—"

"I sure as hell *am* gonna be pissed—"

"But take my word for it, Arlene, you'll be better off if you don't know certain things. It's for your own sake, goddamn it!"

"What things don't I know? *What? What?"* she yelled, eyes blazing.

I said, "About Eric's murder. Dan knows all about Eric's murder, and he's going to tell me about it, Arlene. Aren't you, Dan?"

Arlene looked aghast and said, "No."

Dan sat there and said nothing.

Arlene screamed, then said it again. "No!"

Dan looked at her and said, "I killed Eric."

"You did not!" Arlene shrieked.

"I did, Arlene! I killed Eric!"

"Dan, you've gone over the edge!" Arlene cried out. "You couldn't have killed Eric, and you know it! You were with me the day Eric was killed, and we were in the city picking up a delivery for Liver!"

"No, of course I didn't actually kill him with my own hands!" Dan moaned. "But I might as well have, for chrissakes. I was—I was trying to control everything, and save the paper for Mom and Eric and Janet and me, and—I fucked up, goddamn it."

I said, "So now it's all got to come out, Dan. It's too late to save the paper for the family. The chances are slim that you'll ever find those diamonds in these woods. And even if you did, word is out now, and the jewels would have to be returned to their owners. The best deal you're going to get from now on is, the board votes next month and the paper goes to the decent Griscomb chain and not to god-awful Info-Com."

He said simply, "I know that."

Arlene was rocking on her seat and said, "I can't believe this. I just fucking can't *believe* this, Dan. You never told me those diamonds had anything to do with Eric. I thought they were just some oil profiteer's wife's jewelry, and the fucking diamonds were going for a good cause that would benefit the people!"

"Arlene," I said, "two people died in that robbery, one of them a working man, a member of the international proletariat. Letting that guard live the rest of his life would have been a good people's cause."

"Sure, that sucked, that guard getting killed," Arlene said, "and I'm not saying that two wrongs make a right. But the *Herald* stands up for people like that dead guard, and if the Osbornes lose control of the paper, then it'll start standing up for assholes like big corporations that want to poison the rivers and cut all the trees down. So I agree with what Dan was trying to do. Especially since he didn't even know about the robbery until after it happened."

Another awkward silence. I looked at Dan, and then Arlene did too.

Dan said, almost inaudibly, "I knew about it, Arlene." Then, more loudly: "Of course I knew about it. Come on, Arlene, are you really that naive? I mean—Jesus!"

Arlene slumped and said nothing.

"Was the robbery your idea?" I asked.

Now Dan's face contorted with grief. He said, "No."

Arlene went white and said, "Was it Eric's?"

Dan guffawed once. "God, no. Eric? Don't be absurd."

I said, "What happened, Dan?"

Again another long silence in the woods. "This is the end," Dan finally said. "I'm relieved."

"A lot of people will be."

"I won't," Arlene said, but Dan ignored this.

He took a deep breath and in a shaky voice he said: "Stu Torkildson first came to me last summer and told me the *Herald* would not survive as an Osborne family paper unless we could somehow pay off the Spruce Valley debt. He said the resort project was eating the paper alive. He had already refinanced twice, he said, but the company was only falling further and further behind, and Stu had exhausted all legal means for saving the paper."

When Dan said "legal," he gave us a meaningful look. "Stu said to me," Dan went on, "that I, better than all the other Osbornes, understood how 'questionable means'—his term—are justified by good ends. He mentioned as an example something he knew about that I'd done back in the Movement days in sixty-eight. And then when I agreed to listen to what he had to say, he told me bluntly that he thought Craig would be willing to pull off some moneymaking caper that would rescue the paper.

"Craig's motivation would be getting even with his father by bolstering the position of the liberal Osbornes who controlled the paper. Stu said I shouldn't mention his involvement to Craig because Craig knew Stu and Chester were friends, and that would make Craig suspicious."

I said, "Torkildson actually proposed a jewel robbery?"

Dan laughed sourly and said, "Hell, no. Do you think Stu Torkildson of the Glens Falls Torkildsons is a common criminal? What Stu had in mind was a multimillion-dollar drug deal. He said I had friends in Cuba, and he knew from reading *The Wall Street Journal* that Cuban officials deal coke big-time. This was Stu's idea of keeping the deal respectable."

"So you and Craig would be risking your necks, and Stu would—what?" I asked.

"Stu would do nothing and risk nothing. He told me straight out that if the deal were ever exposed, he would deny any knowledge of it. He only wanted to save the *Herald* for the Osbornes, and he had to save himself for that noble pursuit."

"Right," I said. "The way he saved the *Herald* with the Spruce Valley project."

Arlene blurted out, "And you listened to that flaming asshole, Dan? I can't believe this shit! I just can't believe it!"

"Well, goddamn it, Arlene, how else was I supposed to save the *Herald*? You tell me!"

She shook her head and muttered something inaudible.

I said, "Whose idea was the jewel heist? Craig's?"

"He had this buddy," Dan said, "who'd worked for the hotel and who swore it would be easy to hold the place up in the middle of the night. Nobody would get hurt," Dan said, his pale eyes suddenly full of anguish. "And one job, if they hit the right night, could net over a million in cash and jewels, which I would then fence with my Cuban contacts. Nobody ever guessed that the one robbery alone would produce a haul worth an amount more than equal to the *Herald*'s entire debt. And nobody guessed either that the hotel security man would turn up in the middle of the robbery. According to Craig's buddy, the guard was supposed to be in some other part of the hotel at that hour."

"Did Stu know about the robbery in advance?" I asked.

Dan shrugged. "Only after the fact. He still thought it was going to be a big drug deal, with the laundered cash arriving at the *Herald* by way of a so-called 'loan' from a bank in the Caymans. When he heard that Craig had been arrested for robbery and murder, he wasn't too wild about the news. It was obvious that Stu's going out on a legal limb to save the *Herald* was really to recoup his own battered reputation after the Spruce Valley debacle. A 'world-class' drug deal—that's what Stu said he had in mind—was one thing, but armed robbery was something else, and Stu was on the edge of freaking out when he heard about it."

I said, "And Chester knew none of this?"

"Not in the beginning," Dan said, looking away again.

"But he figured it out," I said. "Craig described that part to me."

Dan nodded grimly. "Fucking greedy, hothead Chester. We knew all along—I knew, Stu knew—not to get Chester involved."

"And Chester never tumbled to the fact that his good pal Stu was the man who had initiated the entire scheme?"

172

"No," Dan said, "Chester found out Craig and I had been spending time together before the robbery. And then when the stolen jewels failed to turn up, Chester was suspicious and went out and confronted Craig at Attica. Chester is such a total asshole. First of all, he threatened to blow open the whole deal if we didn't give him the jewels so that he and June could gain control of the paper. Craig just blew him off.

"Then in May, Chester gets it in his insane head that Eric and I are about to use the diamond money to squeeze him and June out of the paper, and he goes out and confronts Craig a second time. But by then I'd lost the jewels and I was frantically trying to find them up here in the woods, and I was too embarrassed to tell Craig where the jewels went. So when Chester goes out to Attica and says, 'Where are the jewels?' Craig, who's plenty pissed by now, he tells Chester, 'Ask Dan where they are.' "

Arlene said, "Jesus, Dan, what a bunch of fuckheads. Your family sounds like a bunch of people on a daytime TV talk show."

"Every family is a family from a daytime TV talk show!" Dan snapped. "Most families just don't happen to go on television and make fools of themselves in public."

I said, "In the nineties, we're a long way from Tolstoy in these matters, I guess, but let's get back to your interesting narrative, Dan. So Chester then came to you and asked where the jewels were?"

Dan shook his head in disgust. "I told Chester he was nuts and to fuck off, which he did. But what does Chester do next? He goes to Eric. Eric! Eric came to me, and he says, what's this about Craig and me and the jewel robbery? I said, God, Eric, don't be ridiculous, it's just Craig playing head games with Chester. Eric, who was so straight, so naive—Eric just says, oh, okay. And he went back and told Chester that Craig had made up the entire story, none of us had any jewels, and to forget about it."

"It is Craig's belief," I said, "that at that point Chester became so frustrated and angry that he flew into one of his violent rages and killed Eric."

Arlene let loose with another shriek. Dan looked at her and then at me and said quietly, "No. That's not the way it happened."

I said, "Torkildson?"

Dan nodded and Arlene shrieked again.

I said, "How? Why?"

Dan took a deep breath. "By early May," he said, "I was fairly certain I'd never find the jewels out here. I'd spent weeks combing these woods without coming up with a single jewel, and meanwhile the ground cover was getting thicker and thicker."

"You bastard!" Arlene said. "That's the whole month I thought you were out fucking Patsy Livingston again. And here you were up here in the woods looking for diamonds. Dan, you asshole!"

"But the thing was," Dan said, "by that time the paper was up for sale and it already looked as if the board's choice would be either Griscomb or InfoCom. I had finally admitted to Stu that I'd stashed the jewels with Dad's ashes and Eric had unknowingly scattered the contents of the urn up here in the woods. So Stu was getting agitated and he was saying that if we couldn't save the *Herald* for the family—and restore his shattered reputation—then the paper would have to be sold to InfoCom so at least the family could come away with several million. I knew we had the board votes to approve a sale to Griscomb, but Stu started threatening legal action against any board member who blatantly voted against the company's best interests—he said Chester and June would both sue and he would join them—and that's when I panicked and made what turned out to be a terrible, terrible, terrible mistake."

Arlene sat looking frightened but said nothing. No one spoke until Dan took another deep breath, let out a long sigh, and went on.

"I decided to blackmail Stu," Dan said. "I told him that I had lied about Eric throwing the jewels away accidentally. I told him Eric had found the jewels and confronted me, and that I had confessed everything. I said Eric was threatening to go to the police and expose us all, Stu included, but that Eric had agreed to return the jewels to their owners anonymously if Stu threw his support to Griscomb and stopped Chester and June from suing us."

Dan paused and looked off into the woods thoughtfully. I said, "How did Torkildson react?"

"He followed Eric into the woods on the day of Eric's weekly trip to the beaver pond that Eric was writing about in his column and bludgeoned Eric to death. He described the whole thing to me the next day. Stu said he didn't plan to kill anyone else if he could help it, but that after the Spruce Haven bust he was already too embarrassed to show up at the country club on Friday nights, and he would not risk being exposed additionally as an accomplice in a jewel robbery."

Arlene and I sat looking at Dan, who leaned comfortably against his tree but whose eyes were full of terror. Arlene did not exclaim this time, she just sniffled quietly.

I said, "Is there any way it can be proven that Torkildson killed Eric?"

"Sure, I've got the proof," Dan said. "Stu told me he killed Eric with a camera tripod he borrowed from the *Herald*'s picture department. I found the tripod that night and took it home. Stu had washed it off, but there were still traces of blood on it and presumably Stu's fingerprints and other DNA traces."

"Why didn't you turn Torkildson in?" I said. "Dan, the man murdered your brother."

"Well," Dan said, "for one thing, I just wanted to save the paper. I figured Stu would help me do that, considering what I knew. It turned out I was wrong about that. Torkildson is a psychopath. And of course the other thing was, it was my fault. I triggered Stu into killing Eric. I was just as guilty as Stu was."

With that, Dan stood up, walked over, and lifted the tent flap. He went inside, and a thought hit me hard and I stood up abruptly.

I spoke rapidly to Arlene. "He doesn't have a gun or anything in there, does he?"

"No," she said, "Dan's just getting his stash. Sounds like a good idea, huh? Don, I'll bet right about now you could go for a smoke too."

25

Late Saturday afternoon, Bill Stankie arrested Stu Tor-kildson for murder. A magistrate ordered Torkildson held in the Eden County Jail pending forensic tests on the camera tripod Dan had produced. When he was picked up, Torkildson lost his customary cool. Vehemently denying guilt, he railed against the police and the Osbornes. He kept yelling, "After everything I've done for them!" But Stankie said a preliminary lab examination of the tripod supported Dan's story. Plus, it turned out, Torkildson had no alibi for the time of the murder.

Chester had no alibi either, but now he didn't need one. Chester told Stankie that on the morning of Eric's death he had been out examining some woods and pastureland he had been looking at on behalf of the Wal-Mart company, and that's how he'd gotten muddy. He said Pauline's accusation of murder was a result of her mental instability (Craig's malicious phone call to Pauline never came up), and that instability was the subject of an upcoming court hearing.

Chester did admit that he had brought Tacker Puderbaugh back from Tahiti to "play some pranks" on the pro-Griscomb Osbornes. But Tacker and a friend of his from Lake George had "gone too far," Chester said, when they committed arson and then demanded that Chester pay them $150,000 in hush money so that they could open a surfboard rental business on Okinawa.

Both Tacker and his friend were picked up at the friend's house and charged with arson and attempted murder. Janet identified Tacker's friend as the man who attacked her—and later attacked her, Dale, Timmy, and me—on a Jet Ski. At first, Timmy wanted to charge the Jet

Ski maniac with assault too for breaking his foot, but after thinking it over decided to let it go.

For the moment, Chester escaped being slapped behind bars—the DA was considering what charges to bring against him—and Chester's dodging a murder rap was the one disappointment suffered by full-dentured Bill Stankie. Stankie did get to see Torkildson and Tacker occupy adjoining cells (having admitted complicity in the jewel robbery, Dan was released on bond), and Stankie took satisfaction in Tacker's determination to incriminate Chester to the utmost extent. Stankie and the DA were also interested—as was I—in Tacker's assertion that "Mummy"—i.e., June—knew all about Tacker's campaign of terrorism against the pro-Griscomb Osbornes.

When she was informed of all these developments Saturday night, Ruth Osborne seemed unsurprised to learn that Dan, Chester, Tacker, and possibly even June had been involved in criminal activities that grew out of the battle for the soul of the *Herald*. "The Osbornes have always tended toward ruthlessness in support of their causes," she said. But the news of Stu Torkildson's arrest for Eric's murder was even more deeply shocking. Mrs. Osborne began to tremble when Janet told her, and she went up to her room soon after.

"The family always relied on Stu," Janet told Timmy, Dale, and me on the Osborne back porch later that night. "Stu was the man Dad depended on to keep us all both solvent and honest. So to Mom what Stu did must feel like the ultimate betrayal."

"*Was* the ultimate betrayal," Dale said, and we all agreed solemnly with that.

Both Janet and Dale were exhausted from working to salvage belongings from the half of the lake house that remained standing after the fire that Tacker set, and from the shocks of the previous thirty-six hours. They weren't too tired, however, to speculate on the upcoming family board of directors' vote.

"The outcome," Janet said, "is going to depend on which board members are behind bars on September eighth, and which ones will be available to vote. If Dan is still out on bail, that should seal it for Griscomb. If Chester is unable to vote and Tidy comes on to the board, that won't change anything one way or another."

"And certainly your mother should survive the mental competency hearing on Monday," Timmy said. "She's understandably devastated by all this rotten stuff coming out about the family and the fight over the paper. But at this point, anyway, I don't think anybody can deny that her faculties are intact."

"It's also to Ruth's credit," Dale said, "that she hasn't been arrested."

Janet tried to smile but couldn't. "That does seem to be a rarity among Osbornes these days." Janet had spent two hours earlier in the evening giving interviews to reporters from *The New York Times* and the *Boston Globe,* who were preparing big stories on the dissolution of one of the great families of American journalism.

"Have either of you ever been arrested?" Dale asked Timmy and me. It seemed an odd question to ask, but Dale's tight look and bright eyes suggested she had something in mind.

I said, "I've been manhandled a few times in the line of duty by the Albany criminal justice establishment, Dale, and I wear every scar from those encounters as a badge of—not honor, I guess. Bemusement would be more like it, mixed with disgust."

"And what about you, Timmy?" Dale said. "Have you ever been arrested?"

His fiberglass-encased foot bobbed once, his face went white, and sweat popped out on his forehead. Timmy stared at Dale and said, "No. I've never been arrested."

"But *I* have," she said with a look of triumphant contempt. "Haven't I, Timmy?"

He said, "Oh, hell. You were in that ACT-UP group. Oh, hell."

"Yes, I was in that ACT-UP group, oh, hell. In April 1987. I see it all is starting to ring a bell now somewhere deep inside your big, adorable head. Bong, bong, bong."

"Jeez. I felt bad about that. It was after the Health and Human Resources Committee vote on AIDS home-care funding, right?"

"Right you are, Tim."

"And your group thought Assemblyman Lipschutz shouldn't have compromised so much with the Republicans on the budget. You all came over to the office and wouldn't leave—there were forty or fifty of you, as I recall—and you demanded to see Myron."

"Asked nicely to talk to him," Dale said. "Forcefully but nicely."

"No, you demanded to talk to him. Except, as I remember it, he was off in a meeting somewhere with the Speaker."

"That's what you told us at the time. That was all bullshit, of course."

"And you refused to leave the office. Your whole group sat down on the floor, and you said you weren't leaving until Myron heard what you had to say. You were the spokesperson for the group. That's when I left. I went over to the Speaker's office to see if I could pry Myron out of the meeting."

"Uh-huh. So you said."

"And while I was over there, the Capitol Police got word that you were sitting in Myron's office—"

"You *called* them, Timothy! Admit it! You told us we could meet with Assemblyman Lipshutz, and then you went out and called the cops, and we all got arrested. We spent the night in the lockup while you were probably down at the bar at Le Briquet having a good laugh over how you put one over on the dyke and faggot riffraff."

"Dale," Timmy said, "you are wrong, wrong, wrong—as you are every once in a great while. You are as sharp as they come, Dale, but you don't know me. Or Myron Lipshutz. It was Assemblyman Metcalfe, across the corridor, who called the cops on you, and both Myron and I were furious when we came back to the office fifteen minutes later and found out what had happened. It was Myron who got you all a lawyer from Lambda Legal Defense, and it was Myron who, a week later, got another twelve million transferred to AIDS home care from the health administration budget. So if that incident is the cause of your attitude toward me, an adjustment is in order. An apology, I'm sure, is much too much to hope for."

Janet and I each had a swig of beer and watched as Dale carefully considered this. Finally, she said, "How come we never heard this version of events at the time?"

"Because," Timmy said, relaxed and enjoying himself now, "Myron knew he'd never get the extra twelve million if it looked like he was in bed with extortionists. He wanted results, not a lot of—'diarrhea' was Saul Alinsky's term for righteous public explosions that make the demonstrators feel better but achieve nothing lasting. And Myron got results."

Dale sniffed. "The twelve million was a drop in the bucket, speaking of diarrhea. Anyway, without ACT-UP there to remind the legislature of the huge, crying need, the appropriation would have been half what it was."

"That is correct," Timmy said. "ACT-UP and other better-behaved

LA-1999-5-1

groups—each group in its own way—got their points across. They made a big difference."

Dale seemed to relax a bit. She gulped some beer down, then said to Timmy, "Okay, Timothy, my man. You passed the test. You're it."

"Gee whiz, thanks."

" 'Gee whiz.' There's another one of those old-timey exclamations you like to use that we hardly ever hear anymore. Sort of like 'golly gee.' Or 'gee willikers.' I don't suppose, though, that there would be a genetic predisposition to those funny expressions in any of your progeny. So, Timothy, you're it."

Timmy shifted uneasily on his chaise. "What do you mean, 'it'?"

"Janet and I decided several months ago to have a child. I'll be the biological mother. We need a sperm donor, and with Janet's endorsement I've been testing you to see what you're made of. You've passed the test. We need to get to it soon, if you're healthy and it's okay with you, because my clock's running out. And let's not fool around with turkey basters, either. That's so cold and clinical for such an intimate—sacred really—ritual of creation. So whaddya say, Tim, old man? Are you up to it? Ready for some fructification?"

Timmy stared at Dale, and even though it wasn't, his look was that of a man whose hair was standing on end.

Later that night, in June's four-poster, Timmy said, "I hope you're not hurt that they didn't ask you, Don."

I said, "No, their reasons for chosing you are perfectly valid. They think you would be the more loyal and loving and attentive father—or father figure, as Dale insists on calling it—and they're right. If they had asked me, I'd have said no thanks, I've never had the urge. But you knew right away it was something you'd missed in life, and you wanted deeply to do it, even though you'd never realized it before."

"That's right."

"But I'll be interested to be the father-figure-in-law-once-removed, or whatever you call it."

"I know you will."

"I don't know about those names they've picked, though. Shira Osborne-Kotlowicz? Yussie Osborne-Kotlowicz?"

"That's up to them. The names sound fine to me."

"You're not going to press for Sean Callahan-Kotlowicz-Osborne? Or Heather Kotlowicz-Osborne-Callahan?"

"No, I don't care what the name is. I'm just—*exhilarated* is the only word for it—at the idea of creating a human being that's part of me and yet will have a life—a life!—that's all its own."

"I understand that, Timothy. It's not what I want, somehow, but I hear you, and I love it that you're thrilled."

"I am relieved, though, that Dale relented and is willing to use indirect means for the impregnation. I guess I could have managed it, but—really. Geez."

"She's still threatening to jump you some night, though. And, hey, you might be surprised. There might be another revelation in store."

"I have a feeling," Timmy said, "that I would have figured that one out earlier in life. It isn't as though I wasn't encouraged to do so."

"Just think," I said, "you're going to make a human life, and the whole story of that life started with Skeeter back in high school in Poughkeepsie. I'll bet he'll be happy when he hears about it, and even proud."

Timmy became thoughtful at the mention of Skeeter. After a moment, he said, "Maybe Eldon would make a good name for a baby."

"Yeah," I said. "Or Eldona."

We talked for a long time under June's canopy, and decided that one day Eldon or Eldona would be editor of a great newspaper, or—if great newspapers didn't exist anymore in the twenty-first century—a series of feisty pamphlets passed from hand to hand.

Epilogue

Dan Osborne plea-bargained a sentence of one year for his role in the jewel robbery. Tacker Puderbaugh and his Jet Ski-riding accomplice in the arson and the other intimidating "pranks" were convicted and drew sentences of twelve to fifteen years. Chester, charged with conspiracy to commit mayhem, copped a plea and escaped with probation. June got off free too, although the county art museum suspended her for one year as the curator of the annual canoes-at-sunrise show. Parson and Evangeline Bates turned against June and Dick Puderbaugh, and Parson wrote a column in the *Herald* attacking the "liberal judge with his own agenda" who let June off.

Suddenly preoccupied, Chester Osborne canceled the proceeding to have his wife committed. Pauline soon left Edensburg in her Lexus—with a trunk full of bearer bonds, it was rumored—and moved into a hilltop house with a tennis court in La Jolla, California. Arlene Thurber visited Dan once a week in the year he spent in prison and brought homemade brownies for Dan and some of the other inmates.

Stu Torkildson was convicted on Dan's testimony and the DNA evidence on the camera tripod. I visited him in jail while he was awaiting trial, and I asked him how he could have blundered so stupidly in launching the jewel-heist scheme—or big drug deal, as he had originally proposed, according to Dan. I said I thought the Spruce Haven disaster would have dissuaded Torkildson from doing anything hugely risky ever again.

Torkildson gave me his most ingratiating sneer and said, "The drug deal that was going to save the *Herald*—which editorializes against the scourge of drugs, what a laugh—wasn't my idea at all. I argued against it strenuously, Strachey, and if I hadn't given in, against my better judgment, this entire fiasco—Dan's absurd accusation that I murdered Eric, as well as all the rest of it—could have been avoided. I'm not admitting anything in court, mind you. But if I said something to Dan that he construed as my recommending a big drug deal that could save the *Herald,* I will tell you confidentially that I was urged to do so by another party who was determined at any cost to keep the *Herald* in the Osborne family."

He watched me with his eyes that gave nothing away, and I said, "All right, who? Who urged you to save the *Herald* with a big drug deal, Stu?"

"Ruth Osborne. Who else? Doesn't it just sound like Ruth?"

"No."

"Then you don't know Ruth Watson Osborne."

"What proof have you got?"

He shrugged. "None."

"You're lying. You've got the morals of a virus. You're making this up."

He just grinned and slowly shook his gleaming head.

The judge at Ruth Osborne's mental competency hearing found her "understandably sad" but sane enough to remain on the *Herald* board of directors. After the September eighth vote, however, her mental condition deteriorated rapidly, and three months later she suffered a stroke and, after a week of hospitalization, moved into an Edensburg nursing home. I never told Janet what Stu Torkildson had said about the idea of saving the *Herald* through a big drug deal having originated with Mrs. Osborne. I ran it by Timmy, who just waved it away.

The *Herald* board voted, three to two, to sell the paper to Harry Griscomb. The deal was consummated within days. Griscomb assumed the *Herald*'s huge debt, so each Osborne shareholder received, after taxes, just $12,114. Janet said hers would help pay for rebuilding the lake house, and adding a nursery. The other shareholders no doubt spent theirs on legal bills.

The following spring two things happened. Erica McCaslin Kotlowicz-Osborne was born on May 30th at Edensburg County Hospital. Skeeter was there—his T-cell numbers were ominous but his health was holding steady, and he'd returned to work for the New York State Forest Service. Timmy was there too, pacing in the waiting room while Skeeter and I played hearts. Janet was present for the delivery—a highly unorthodox arrangement, hospital officials insisted, but they weren't about to tangle with Janet and Dale.

The other event that May was this: Harry Griscomb Newspapers suffered a financial near-collapse and the third generation of Griscombs seized control of the chain and sold it to the new newspaper division at United States Tobacco. Janet was fired a day later, as were two-thirds of the paper's reporters and all the copy editors. Tidy Osborne Puderbaugh was named publisher of the *Herald*—"to maintain the respected Osborne family traditions," the new owner said—and a new editor was brought in from the Maryville, Missouri, *Epworth-Tribune*. The features and standards that had made the *Herald* great soon vanished from its pages—but it did gain a bridge column.